CYNTHIA HICKEY

Collision Course
Overcoming Evil
Book 6

Cynthia Hickey

DEDICATION

Thank you to all my readers who anxiously await the
next story in this romantic suspense series

CHAPTER ONE

Lacey Baxter stared in horror at the surveillance photos in her hand. When her dear Aunt Ruth died, Lacey had put off cleaning out the attic as long as possible. Now, she wished she had put it off longer. Life had hit a decline it might never pull out of.

Aunt Ruth jogged every day, despite being fifty-five years old. It was inconceivable that she would have fallen to her death on the trail she ran five days out of seven. The photos in Lacey's hand showed someone had been watching not only Aunt Ruth, but Lacey as well.

What did she ever do to require someone watching her? She glanced up from the dusty box toward the attic window. Aunt Ruth had mentioned she thought someone was following her. Lacey had overheard her talking to Uncle Ben late one night. When she'd walked into the room, they'd stopped, her uncle giving her his common sneer when he bothered to pay her any attention at all.

Her breath came in gasps. Aunt Ruth had been murdered, and Lacey could very well be next. She shoved the photos back into the envelope. She'd go through the rest of it at home.

"Lacey?" Uncle Ben's voice drifted up the attic steps.

"Be right down." She folded the manila envelope and stuffed it under her sweatshirt. There was little danger of Uncle Ben giving her a hug and discovering the photos. After all, he hadn't laid a hand on her since marrying her aunt two years ago, not that she minded.

She climbed down the stairs and faced the man she liked the least of anyone she knew. "I'm just going through Aunt Ruth's things. It will take a while."

"Don't let me stop you." He loosened the crimson tie around his throat.

"No, I'll come back tomorrow. It's a noisy, messy job." She tried to move past him.

His hand shot out and gripped her wrist. "What's the hurry? Join me for dinner. It's been lonely the last few weeks." His gaze raked her body.

"I've got to go." She yanked free and dashed from the house. His meaning was clear. He meant to replace Aunt Ruth with Lacey.

Why? There was no love lost between them. She shuddered and slipped behind the wheel of her Jeep. Uncle Ben watched from the living room window. She shivered again and backed from the driveway as a cold rain mixed with sleet began to fall.

If Aunt Ruth had indeed been murdered, had he done it? Lacey blinked away the tears and hurried to her small bungalow on the outskirts of town. Once home, she hurried inside, tossing the envelope on the table. She set a pot of water on the stove to boil before dumping out the contents of the envelope.

Pushing aside the photos, she unfolded a sheet of paper and sat down to read. Aunt Ruth had suspected Uncle Ben of trying to kill her. She stated in her letter that she had stumbled across incriminating evidence that would ruin Uncle Ben's reputation in the town. The evidence was located in a small locked chest in Grandpa's farmhouse.

Shock rippled through Lacey. The paper fell from her trembling hands. She needed to go to Grandpa's house right away. If Uncle Ben was responsible for Aunt Ruth's death, then he had no business walking the streets as an upstanding citizen of Oak Grove.

She shoved the paper and photos back into the envelope and raced to her bedroom to toss warm clothing in a small suitcase. She grabbed some toiletries and her camera, laid the envelope on top, and zipped the case closed. She would find a way to put those responsible for her aunt's death behind bars, even if it meant dying to do so.

She was almost out of her room when she noticed the light blinking on her answering machine. She pressed the button. An electronically garbled voice warned, "Get out of town. He's after you." Lacey scribbled the phone number on a slip of paper, shoved it into the pocket of her jeans, and deleted the message before rushing into the hall.

Headlights pierced the front window curtains. Lacey plastered her back against the wall and peered out. Uncle Ben. She gripped her suitcase tighter. If she left the front door unlocked, and escaped out the back, perhaps she could get away before he caught her. He'd search the house before determining she had fled. She turned the door lock.

She dashed through the kitchen, turned off the gas to the stove, and barreled out the back door. His calls rang out behind her.

"Lacey, I think you have something I need."

How did he know?

"I saw it on your face. Come back, girl. We could make an excellent team. There's no reason for you to suffer your aunt's fate."

The winter's air cut into her lungs, making her gasp. She skidded to a halt beside her car and tossed the suitcase into the backseat. His car blocked hers, but desperate times called for desperate measures. She slid behind the wheel, turned the key in the ignition, and sped through her yard, leaving tire tracks through the dead grass.

Once on the road, she sped toward the highway.

~

Lacey swiped the tears away with the back of her hand. Night had fallen, obscuring her vision while the clouds released their burden of rain.

The road dipped and she hit the brakes. The car slid. Her foot pumped. The Jeep didn't slow. Bright headlights behind her made seeing even more difficult. A horn blared. Her uncle was behind her.

She fought the steering wheel as a sharp turn sent her into a spin. She struggled to keep her Jeep on the slick road. Her windshield wipers tapped out a steady rhythm against the sleet pelting her window. She couldn't see a thing. Why hadn't she waited until daylight to head to the cabin? She could have taken refuge in a motel. Driving while fatigue coated your limb was never a good idea. Yet the sense of urgency wouldn't leave her.

The vehicle spun like the tea cup ride at Disneyland. Lacey screamed and tightened her grip. Which way was she supposed to turn the wheel? She yanked to the right and slid. A truck loomed in front of her window. She screamed and wrestled harder with the wheel.

Screeching filled the night before she crashed through a wooden fence. The seatbelt dug into her neck and chest. She shoved the airbag out of her way, coughing after inhaling the white powder it released.

Several shoves with her shoulder against the crinkled door and Lacey fell in the mud outside her car. She squinted to make out the truck she'd scraped against. Headlights glimmered faintly through the night's haze. How could she not have seen the lights?

With her hands slipping and dampness seeping through the knees of her jeans, she crawled to the other vehicle. As she got closer, she noticed the jack and flat tire next to it. Where was the driver?

She hadn't hit him, had she? Please, God, no. She scrambled to her feet; her breath coming in gasping rasps. She glanced behind the wheel. No one sat slumped over on the front seat. Maybe the truck was abandoned. No, not with the lights left on.

Lacey gripped her hair with both hands, not caring

if she smeared mud through the long strands. Something wasn't right. She studied the discarded flat tire. A new one leaned against the fender. Her gaze slid to the road. If a person squatted here, and an out-of-control vehicle careened toward them … there! In the ditch. Lacey slid down the embankment and came to a stop beside a man.

Dark hair lay matted to his face from the rain. Several inches of water sloshed around him as the icy drizzle turned into a steady stream of rain from heaven. Lacey dropped to her knees and placed two fingers to his neck. A steady thump greeted her, dispelling some of her fear. How was she going to get him back to her Jeep?

A cry came from the cab of the truck, freezing Lacey more effectively than the winter rain. When the sound came again, she climbed back to the road and stumbled to the truck. She shoved the driver's seat forward. Her knees sagged when she spotted the child in the backseat. When she caught sight of Lacey, the little girl wailed louder.

"Shush, baby, shush." Lacey unbuckled the child and clutched it to her chest. "It's okay."

Was it okay? Why hadn't she charged her cell phone? She propped the little girl on her hip and rummaged in a pile of fast food containers with the other. Bingo! Her fingers wrapped around a cell phone.

She punched in 9-1-1 and squeezed the phone to her ear to try and block out the child's cries.

"9-1-1, what is your emergency?"

"I, uh, ran my car into a ditch. I think I might've hit somebody. He's lying in a ditch that's quickly filling up with water." He was going to drown and it would be all

Lacey's fault.

"Is he alive?"

"Yes."

"What's your location?"

"I don't know. The freeway, somewhere. Between mile markers 101 and 102, I think." Tears burned the back of Lacey's throat. She should've paid more attention. "Please hurry. There's a screaming toddler here, and I don't have anything to give her." Not to mention the threat racing her way down the highway, if her instincts were right. If he found her alone with a small child…she shook her head refusing to go there.

"Please stay calm and don't hang up. Help is on the way."

"Okay." Lacey shoved the phone in her pocket. She had to check on the man she'd hit. She glanced at the little girl in her arms. "No help for it, sweetie. You've got to come with me."

She slipped and slid her way down the bank until she landed in ankle deep water. Thankfully, the man's head rested on the incline. She set the little girl out of reach of the water. She'd still be cold and wet from the rain, but if Lacey didn't help the man, he'd drown. She glanced up the embankment where a car's headlights slashed through the rain. He was here. The car idled for a moment and pulled away.

~

"Mister? Please, wake up."

John Canyon opened his eyes to the sight of a strange and very muddy woman staring down at him. Breaking through the fuzz in his brain, was the shrill sounds of a child's screams. Meagan!

He pushed the woman to the side and climbed up

the embankment to gather his niece in his arms. The poor thing had been through enough. She didn't need to be sitting in the cold rain.

John had just returned from the temporary foster home where his niece had lived for the week since the death of his brother who was her father. He pulled his niece into his arms and turned to glare at the woman. "You almost ran over me."

"Almost? Thank God." She sagged and knelt in a puddle. "I thought I'd hit you." She pulled his phone from her pocket and handed it out to him. "9-1-1 is on the phone. You're bleeding."

John put a hand to the knot on his head. His hand came away sticky. "I hit my head on a rock." Foolish woman. If she couldn't handle the mountain roads, she shouldn't be driving in the winter rain.

He struggled back to the shoulder of the road where an ambulance and a squad car pulled up, their blinking lights reflected in the rain puddles. A first responder rushed to John's side, and then led him to the ambulance while another went to help the woman up the hill.

Her older model Jeep hung over the embankment, pieces of the guard rail sticking out of the fender. She wouldn't be driving that vehicle any time soon. She was lucky to be walking.

A police officer called a tow truck. John hoped he could convince the tow truck driver to replace his flat. Someone put a warm blanket around his shoulders. He sat and cradled his niece as his head wound was cleaned and bandaged.

"You should go to the hospital and get checked out," the paramedic said. "You probably have a concussion."

"I'm fine. Nothing a goodnight's rest won't cure." He watched as the woman sloshed through the ankle-deep water toward him.

"I'm so sorry. My name is Lacey Baxter. I promise to get my insurance information to you as soon as it's safe to go in my Jeep."

Despite his anger at her carelessness, John's heart softened at the pained look on her face. "We'll all be fine." She might be pretty, once the mud was cleaned out of her hair and off her face. "Do you live around here?"

"I'm headed to my family's cabin." She perched on the ambulance bumper next to him. "It's just up the road."

"So you're my neighbor." Great. The one house within walking distance belonged to the woman who'd almost killed him. "I'm new to town, but I'm living at the farm up the road."

Lacey nodded. "If you'll give me your keys, I'll drive you home. It won't hurt me to walk from there. I'm wet and muddy as it is."

"I'll manage."

"Pardon me if it's none of my business, but you hit your head. You probably shouldn't be driving. What if you pass out behind the wheel? Think of your daughter."

"My niece."

Lacey was right. He shouldn't drive anywhere for at least a day. The thought of accepting help from her was like a stake in his side. He could just as easily ask one of the police officers to drive him home, but for some reason, he couldn't turn down the earnest offer. The woman wanted to make amends in any way possible. Who was he to deny her?

"We'll have to wait for the tire to be changed."

She nodded and watched as the tow truck arrived and pulled her Jeep out of the railing. "I love that thing. I hope they can fix it." She jumped to her feet. "I'll ask them to change your tire." And then, she splashed her way to the workers.

John shook his head. She definitely had a take-charge attitude. Well, she could keep it to herself. He wanted to be left alone, so he and Meagan could get used to his brother no longer being around. The last thing he needed was a woman who would knock on his door to try and make up for almost running him over.

A few minutes later, she was back. "They'll get us up and running." She wiggled her fingers until he dropped the keys into her hand. "I'll drop you off, then stop back by in the morning to see how you're doing."

John groaned and gave the blanket back to the paramedic. It promised to be a long night.

A car idled at the side of the road, and then raced off with a screech of tires. Wonderful. A rubbernecker.

"Hey, John." The tow truck driver jogged to his side.

"Hey, Roy. Can you fix my tire?" So, the high school shortstop had taken over his father's business. He'd thought Roy would head to college on a scholarship. Most likely a lot of things had changed while John was away.

"Sure, let me get this Jeep out of the way, and I'll have you headed home in a jiffy."

A black suburban slowed as it passed the accident, its windows too dark for John to see inside. Stupid rubberneckers could cause another wreck if they didn't move on.

Meagan's sobs had subsided, but the little girl shivered from the cold and damp. There would be dry clothes in her suitcase next to her car seat. "Come on, sweetie. Let's get you dry. Maybe there's another juice box, too."

Lacey watched as Roy crawled under the Jeep, not seeming to mind the weather.

Maybe the woman really was crazy. It might not be a good idea to let her drive him home. With a child to care for, John needed to be hesitant about letting strangers around her.

Roy slid from under the Jeep and said something to Lacey. She whirled to face John, her eyes wide in her pale face.

It was none of John's business. He continued to change Meagan out of her wet clothes and found a drink for her, and then strapped her back into her seat.

"John." Roy jogged to his side. "There's something I think you should know."

"Yeah?"

"This woman's brake lines were cut. Just like your brother's. Isn't that a strange coincidence?"

CHAPTER TWO

Lacey dropped off a silent John and headed down the road to her cabin after promising she'd call when she arrived safely. She'd have to think of some way to thank her neighbor for the use of his truck. She'd return the vehicle in the morning, maybe with a plate of cookies, if she could get to the store.

She lugged her suitcase into the house, locked the front door, and then set the case in the first bedroom. She tossed her purse on the bed.

She pulled out the photos of her uncle in incriminating poses with a strange woman and the ones of Aunt Ruth jogging. Poor Aunt Ruth. Lacey never could accept the fact that her death had been an accident. She plopped onto the bed, not caring about her wet clothes. Something was rotten. She would need to search for the chest as soon as the trembling from her accident subsided.

Who had called her earlier that evening and warned her to get out of town? She wasn't usually prone to panic attacks, but something in the muffled voice had sent shivers down her spine. Once she added the phone call to the cold glances her uncle had sent her way during the funeral, and the finding of the envelope with the pictures, she couldn't get away fast enough.

Aunt Ruth buried a week ago today, and now Lacey had raced away from her home like an anxious worrywart, when all she wanted was time to grieve.

She fell back onto the bed and stared at the ceiling. Wooden beams supported the roof and added a rustic feel to the place. Once upon a time, Lacey had loved visiting the cabin, now it felt like a prison. A place she had to come to in order to hide away.

She studied the pictures again. What were the fields of green in the one? She didn't recognize the plant, but she did recognize the barrel of a gun showing in one corner of the photo. What was her uncle involved in? What could cause a man who seemed to love Aunt Ruth to kill her, as Lacey now feared he had?

Confusion clouded her mind. Maybe she could think more clearly in the morning. Make some sense out of cut brake lines and dirty pictures.

She pulled John's card from her pocket and reached for the phone beside the bed. She dialed his number on the old fashioned rotary phone. "John? It's Lacey Baxter."

"Hello. No, Meagan, it's too late for ice cream."

Lacey smiled at the reminder that life did proceed as normal for some people. "I've made it safely home. Thank you again for the use of your truck. My grandfather has an old Ford in the garage. I'll bring yours back tomorrow and see if I can't get the Ford running until my car is out of the shop."

"No hurry. I don't have anywhere to go for a day or two. Your car will be fixed by then."

"I guess it pays to know people."

"I guess it does. Good evening, Miss Baxter." He chuckled, the sound rumbling through the phone like far off thunder during a summer storm.

"Goodnight." She hung up and stared out the window. The rain had stopped, and gauzy clouds drifted across the face of the moon.

She'd had no trouble taking time away from her job as a professional photographer. After all, they automatically gave a week for the death of a family member, and were more than willing to give her extra time to settle her aunt's affairs. *Oh, Aunt Ruth.*

Tears started fresh, soaking her hair and the blanket under her head. What happened to you? Lacey vowed to get to the bottom of her aunt's death. She couldn't believe that her aunt would fall off the path she ran on every day. No, she'd been pushed, and Lacey intended to prove it. She'd take the night to mourn, but come morning, she planned to begin investigating dear Uncle Ben.

It shouldn't be too hard, even with him chasing her out of town. Lacey had a key to her aunt's place and lots of things to shift through before Uncle Ben tossed anything of importance. She'd go while the man was at work and pray he didn't have anyone watching the house.

Why would he? As far as he knew, Lacey had run like a scared rabbit. Maybe he wouldn't consider such a person any kind of serious threat. He would be wrong on that account. Lacey would do whatever needed doing to get to the bottom of her aunt's death.

She shuffled to the bathroom and turned on the shower. Undressing and dropping her clothes in a pile on the scuffed bathroom tiled floor, she tested the water for warmth. She'd forgotten how cold the cabin got in the winter. In the morning, she'd need to locate the space heater for the bathroom.

She stepped under the hot spray of the shower as her telephone rang. If it was important, they'd call her cell phone. Wait. No one knew she'd fled to the cabin except John, and she hadn't given him the landline number. Nor had she charged her cell phone. She strained her ears to hear, breathing a sigh of relief when the phone went silent after three rings. A telemarketer, most likely.

Had Aunt Ruth told Uncle Ben about the cabin? They'd only been married for two years, and as far as Lacey knew, they'd never spent time up there.

Lacey stepped out of the shower and caught a glimpse of herself. Dark circles ringed her eyes. Fatigue was etched in every line of her face. She needed sleep and needed it in the worse way. After donning an oversized tee-shirt and cotton pajama pants, she slid under the quilt on the bed and turned down the light. She'd left the kitchen light on, something she always did at the cabin. When dark fell in the woods, it fell heavily with no street lamps to cut the inkiness.

As she settled in, the house showed its age in creaks and groans. The moon cast silver paths of light over the worn floorboards. The bare branches of an oak tree outside the window scratched skeletal fingers over the glass. Lacey smiled and burrowed deeper under the covers. She'd almost forgotten how much she loved the place.

What was John Canyon's story? The man had been understandably angry about almost being run over, but Lacey had apologized profusely. Still, despite his apparent lack of patience with her, he'd allowed Lacey the use of his truck.

Sadness had shadowed his eyes, even while he held the darling little girl. There'd been no mention of a wife, only John's calling the little girl his niece. There was a story there. One that Lacey would like to dig into, once she solved the mystery of her aunt's death.

~

John closed the door on Meagan's room and headed downstairs to his office. He looked forward to an hour or two of quiet time after putting the little girl down for the night.

"Is there anything else you need from me?" The nanny, a sour-faced middle-aged woman with the personality of a turnip, peeked into his study. "If not, I'll head home and see you in the morning."

"That will be all, Susan. Thanks for staying later than usual."

She nodded and stomped down the hall.

John flipped through the pile of papers on his desk. So, Lacey's brakes had been cut, too. He leaned back in his chair, the leather squeaking in protest. What could the woman possibly have in common with his brother?

As a Drug Enforcement Officer, it was John's nature to be suspicious when something didn't make sense, and today's events definitely fit the bill.

A beautiful woman almost runs over him, and then they discover she had something dangerously in common with John's deceased brother. His job experience didn't allow for believing in coincidences.

He picked up a pen from his desk and tapped it against the polished wood. He lived on a rarely traveled road, yet Lacey Baxter almost killed him, and another car had idled from the blacktop, seemingly interested in what was happening below. Another so-called coincidence? It didn't add up.

He reached for the phone and called the local police department. "Sergeant Lawson, here."

"Sergeant, this is DEA Officer Canyon. I'd like to request further investigation into the death of Jason Canyon."

"On what grounds?"

"On the grounds that I was almost killed by another person with cut brake lines."

"I don't have any record of that."

John puffed out his cheeks, then expelled a harsh breath. "I'm sure the report hasn't been written yet. It happened about two hours ago."

"The Wood Lakes Department is understaffed, sir. I'm sure you can appreciate that. You're brother's death isn't a priority at this time."

John snapped the pen between two of his fingers, staining them with blue ink. It might not be a priority for them, but it sure was for John. "I'm not satisfied with that answer."

"Look, officer, you're on a leave of absence. While I appreciate your concern, take the time needed to get your brother's affairs taken care of, and I'll move your brother's case up in the caseload. That's the best I can do."

John hung up the phone and shot to his feet. The sudden movement made him light-headed, and he leaned against the desk for support. His head pounded from hitting it on the rock. He opened a desk drawer and withdrew a bottle of aspirin. He took out a bottle of water from a small fridge he kept in his office and downed two of the small white pills.

Rain started again. John stared and wondered if it would turn to more ice by morning. Oftentimes the mountain roads became impassable during the winter months. He'd need to find time to head to town and stock up on supplies.

Did his new neighbor know that she could be stranded for days once snow fell? He'd have to tell her when she returned his truck. Maybe she'd reconsider spending too much time in her cabin and head back to where she'd come from. He shouldn't feel antagonistic toward her for the accident. After all, it wasn't her fault, but he couldn't help the bite of anger when he thought of her.

Meagan whimpered from the next room. Probably one of her nightmares. The little darling was prone to them since the death of her parents. John strained his ears to hear whether he needed to check on her. When no other sound came his way, he headed for the shower.

Clean and wearing loose basketball shorts and a clean tee-shirt, John headed for the kitchen. He hated eating right before bed, but his stomach complained that he hadn't eaten since lunch, and that was hours ago.

He quickly put together a sandwich and gazed out the kitchen window. He could barely make out the glow from Lacey's cabin. Did she sleep with a light on? He'd thought for sure she'd be asleep by then.

None of his business. He carried his late supper into the living room and turned on the news. Nothing was said of the accident. Good. The last thing he needed was nosy reporters putting the pieces together.

The need to dig further into Jason's death nagged at him. It wouldn't be easy with a small child. Maybe John should consider hiring a full-time nanny. At least for the time being. The house had plenty of bedrooms, and he wouldn't have to worry if his investigating kept him out late.

He finished the sandwich and the water and headed to his room next to Meagan's and climbed into bed. The sheets were cool on his skin. He plumped his pillow and rolled to his side.

A moving slide of the events leading to his diving into the ditch played on the back of his eyelids. The anxiety he'd experienced at seeing his niece in the arms of a stranger. The horror on the beautiful woman's face. Oh, yeah. He'd noticed how pretty she was even with her hair hanging in wet strands on each side of her face. He thought her hair might be blond, but it was hard to tell in the dark.

One thing he did know—he'd have to make sure she kept her distance. He didn't have time to worry about her while raising his niece and wondering what trouble Jason had gotten into. Let the police worry about Lacey Baxter's brakes.

John had enough on his mind.

CHAPTER THREE

Lacey stepped outside and promptly went back to the warm kitchen. Hopefully, the day would warm up before she attempted another drive on the icy road. She didn't think John would be happy if she crashed his truck.

Instead, she decided to look for the chest. With a cup of coffee in hand, she headed for the small extra bedroom Grandpa had used as his office.

Bookshelves containing new and old books covered one wall. Between some vintage first-print editions, set an ornate chest about half the size of a bread box. It had to be what Aunt Ruth had mentioned. A small gold lock dangled from the chest.

Where had Lacey seen a key small enough to fit? She sipped her drink, burning her tongue, and set the mug on the tabletop. Her aunt's charm bracelet had a small gold key dangling from it. Problem was, the bracelet was still at her aunt's house.

Lacey bit the inside of her cheek. She needed to

make a trip to the house, preferably when Ben wasn't there and before the first snow fell. With her aunt dead, she didn't need to call him uncle anymore. The man had been a family member in name only as far as she was concerned.

Her cell phone jingled. One glance at the number showed that a phone replacement would be number two on Lacey's to-do list. She turned the phone off. Ben could call until springtime, and she wouldn't answer. Not until she found out for sure whether he killed Aunt Ruth.

Grabbing a coat from the rack beside the front door, Lacey again braved the frigid weather and crunched across frozen ground to the separate garage. Grandpa always kept a set of keys for the old Ford in his rusty toolbox. She fished for them and stared at the primer-gray beast of a truck.

"Well, old gal, let's see if you still have what it takes." Lacey hopped into the front seat and pumped the gas pedal. After turning the key and several frantic whines of the engine, it turned over. "That's the way we do it." Now, she could return John's truck and still have a way to get around until her vehicle was fixed.

She left the garage and headed for the house. A dark sedan drove slowly past and turn-around at the end of the road. Uneasiness prickled Lacey's skin and she increased her pace, almost running into the house. When the car drove by without stopping, she laughed. What a scaredy-cat she'd turned out to be. No one knew where she was, least of all Ben.

After retrieving the keys to John's truck, she grabbed her purse and drove down the road. A woman walked up the path and into the front door of his house.

Maybe he was married, after all. Lacey pulled into the driveway and cut the engine.

John met her at the front porch. "I didn't need it back right away."

"That's all right." She handed him the keys. "I got my grandpa's old Ford running. She'll suffice for now." She bit the inside of her cheek and studied his strong face. Chocolate brown hair, cut a little longer than military cut contrasted with dark blue eyes. A strong chin and chiseled lips. The woman she'd spotted entering the house was a lucky woman.

"Tell your wife thank you for me." Lacey shoved her hands into her pockets and turned to leave.

"I'm not married."

"Oh." Well, it was none of her business who came and went. "Thanks again."

She strode across the yard, avoiding the more slick areas. When she reached the road, she glanced back to see John still watching from his porch. She shrugged. What a strange man. Handsome, but very different from anyone she'd ever met before. Getting him to talk was like prying a bone from a starving dog.

She trudged along, keeping to the ditch so as to not slip on the icy blacktop. The sound of a car engine reached her ears, and she turned. Coming around the bend was the same sedan that had passed her house earlier. It increased its speed and roared toward her.

Lacey leaped out of the way and sprinted across the empty pasture between her cabin and John's farm. Her breath plumed in front of her. A stitch caught in her side, and she paused to glance behind her.

The car had slowed, unable to follow across the ditch. Instead, it drove slowly down the road toward the cabin. Someone did know Lacey was there.

She burst through the front door, locking it behind her. What should she do? She had nowhere else to go. So far, the occupant of the sedan made no move to confront her. Was it possible they were sent only to observe her? To see what she knew and intended to do?

Somewhere in the house was Grandpa's revolver. He'd taught Lacey how to clean and load it years ago. She wasn't a good shot, but maybe it would be enough of a deterrent if someone should break into the cabin.

After searching the closets in the two bedrooms, and under the beds, she found the locked metal box under the kitchen sink. Dear old Grandpa. Dementia had set in later in his life. He'd most likely stuck the box there and forgot about it. Lacey dug in the silverware drawer until she located the key and also found a small gold one that looked as if it might fit the chest. She unlocked the box and pulled out the .357 Magnum.

It sat heavy in her hand. She pointed it at the back door. A face appeared in the window. Lacey screamed.

~

"Whoa." John ducked, falling to his knees on the stoop. "I came to make sure you made it home okay. Is everything all right?" What was wrong with the woman? She was definitely crazy. He would need to tread carefully around her. Maybe she was mixed up in his brother's death and not completely as a victim.

"I'm so sorry." Lacey pushed open the door. "It isn't loaded."

"How was I supposed to know that?" He glowered and brushed off the knees of his jeans. "I can see you made it home all right. I'll be going now."

"Wait."

She took her top lip between her teeth, distracting John from the point that he should be angry with her for pointing a gun at him.

"How much traffic does this road get?"

"Hardly any, why?" He cocked his head.

Worry lines formed between her eyes. "No reason." She glanced toward the road.

"Is something bothering you? Is that why you have the gun?" He put a hand on the door and stepped up.

She stopped him before he could enter. "I'm sure it's nothing, but there's this car…no, it's nothing." She forced a smile. "Thank you for checking on me."

"Are you in trouble?" John peered over her shoulder and lowered his voice. "Nod if you're not alone."

She shook her head. "I'm fine. It's really nothing but my over-active imagination."

What would she do if he pushed his way in? He eyed the gun in her hand. Should he call the police? She wasn't breaking the law as far as he could tell. "Let me in."

"I'm getting ready to go to town and buy groceries." She turned and grabbed a purse off the counter. "In fact, I'm leaving right now." She dropped the gun in her purse.

"Wonderful. I'm headed there myself. I'll give you a ride." He almost asked her if she had a permit to carry a concealed weapon, but weighed the dangers of not having a weapon against the possibility of a ticket. The ticket lost.

He wasn't any more excited about her company than she seemed to be to about his, but his gut told him she was in immediate danger, and he'd learned a long time ago to listen to his instincts. Why would she put an unloaded gun in her purse? His neighbor was a mystery, for sure. "Shouldn't you load the gun? It's no use to you if it's empty."

She grabbed a handful of bullets and tossed them inside her purse. Looking as if she was headed to a guillotine, Lacey stepped outside and pulled the door closed. "Thank you. A ride would be appreciated."

As they headed to his home, John studied Lacey out of the corner of his eye. The winter sun shot strands of fire through her hair. He'd been right about her being a blond, but there were also strands of red. Dark blue eyes flickered from the road, then behind them, and back to the road. Who was she looking for?

When they reached his house, John held the front door open and allowed Lacey to enter first. The nanny crossed the hall, a tray of juice and cookies in her hands. "Are you leaving, Mr. Canyon?"

"Yes, I'm headed to town." He eyed the sugar-laden snack. How many times did he need to tell her that he wanted Meagan to cut down on her sugar intake? He mentally added to his to-do list that he would look for a full-time, live-in nanny. Hopefully, one that would also teach Meagan pre-school activities.

"Let me get my keys and we can go." He grabbed them from a tray on the foyer table before entering the living room where Meagan sat engrossed in cartoons. He planted a kiss on the top of her head. "I'll be back in a little while, sweetheart. You be good, okay?"

Meagan nodded without dragging her attention away from the exploits of an animated girl and her dog. She watched too much television.

He sighed and motioned for Lacey to follow him

into the garage. "I need to replace the spare while we're in town. I'll drop you at the grocery store and pick you up an hour later. There will be snow soon. You'll need to stock up. Will that work?"

"Perfect." She climbed into the passenger seat and snapped her seatbelt into place before placing her purse on the floorboard. "Do you know anyone that drives a dark sedan?"

"I don't think so, why?" He backed the truck from the garage.

"No reason." She stared out the window.

"If you would tell me what's going on, I might be able to help." He shook his head and drove onto the blacktop. Something ate at her enough to cause him anxiety just by being in close proximity.

Her mood dampened the brightness of the day. John shivered against a sudden chill. Maybe he should have let her go to town alone. Did he really want to get drawn into a stranger's problems? He was on a leave of absence. Meagan needed to be his top priority. Not a pretty, but sullen, neighbor.

Leaving her to her thoughts, John focused on the road ahead, skirting around icy spots. They definitely didn't need a repeat of last night. He pumped the brakes to make sure they were in good working order. He snorted. Now, he was paranoid.

With a possible good reason. Jason's and Lacey's brakes cut? He didn't buy it. He cut her a sideways glance. He'd never met her before. What connection could she possibly have to his brother?

Could one of John's prior drug busts have come back to haunt him? Wouldn't he have remembered a woman of Lacey's beauty if he'd run across her before?

He was missing something.

"Well?" Lacey glared at him.

"Well what?"

"You've been staring at me for five minutes. Do I have something on my face? Is my hair messy?"

"I'm just wondering if we've met before." He tightened his grip on the steering wheel. He should have been more subtle.

"Not that I know of."

"Have you ever met a Jason Canyon?"

"No. Your brother?" At John's nod, she continued. "What does he do for a living?"

"He was a private investigator. He died in a car accident two weeks ago."

"I'm sorry for your loss, and I've never had need of an investigator before." She turned to stare back out the window. "I buried my aunt last week. She raised me since I was ten." She started to say something else, but sighed instead.

They were both grieving. Most likely that explained Lacey's strange behavior.

They came to a T in the road, and John turned his blinker to signal they were going left. Lacey gasped and straightened in her seat.

John glanced in the rearview mirror. A dark sedan followed close to the truck's bumper.

CHAPTER FOUR

"**A**re they going to hit us?" Lacey turned as far as her seatbelt would allow.

"Not if I can help it." John accelerated, taking the truck rocketing down the road.

Lacey gripped the handle to her right. "That car has been driving up and down our road since last night. I think it followed me here." Ben drove a Suburban, but it wouldn't be too difficult for him to get his hands on another vehicle.

John glanced out the corner of his eye. "You and I need to have a serious discussion."

"Can it wait until we get home?"

He nodded, focusing back on the road. "I'll go with you to the grocery store, then we'll go together to get me a new spare. If that car is following you, I don't want you alone."

Despite relief in knowing she might not have to face the danger alone, she didn't want to involve an innocent bystander. "I can't let you get involved. This is my business."

A muscle ticked in his jaw. "When you hear my story, you may feel that is no longer true. You couldn't have picked a worse person to almost run over."

Her blood chilled as if the wind outside had gone to the bone. Who was this man and could she trust him? Now that she had the box, which she had yet to open because of John's surprise visit, maybe she should flee again. If she kept moving, perhaps she could bring her aunt's killer to justice and stay alive at the same time.

She kept glancing over her shoulder. The sedan kept pace with them. "Can you lose them?"

"Wouldn't do much good. Oak Grove is a small town. They'll find the truck easy enough. We need to stay in a populated place and make a visit to the police."

"They won't listen. My uncle is a powerful man." Lacey kept her gaze on the car following them. "If it's him, they'll never make a move against him."

"Who is your uncle?"

"Benjamin Harper."

He stiffened. "The mayor's brother? You do know how to stir the pot, don't you? Hopefully, they'll listen to me."

"What makes you so special?" Lacey settled back in her seat. It was obvious the sedan was going to follow, not crash.

"I'm a Drug Enforcement Agent on a leave of absence."

She glanced at him in surprise. "Here? In Oak Grove?"

He shook his head. "No, I only live here for now. I'm from Los Angeles, originally."

He was a long way from home. She glanced out the passenger window. Could she trust him? It would be nice not to have to bring down her uncle on her own. She needed to look in her aunt's box before making any decisions.

John parked in front of the grocery store, the sedan parked a few spots over. Lacey squinted, trying to make out who was behind the heavily tinted windows. Nothing. She kept close to John's side and entered the store.

Other customers had the same idea. The place was packed with people stocking up on nonperishables and water. Lacey grabbed a couple of cheap flashlights and batteries, then headed for the canned food aisle.

Soon, she had enough soup to last two weeks. She added bread, peanut butter, and jelly. With several cases of bottled water and the makings of tea and coffee, she would be fine if they were snowed in and the electricity went out. Grandpa had a generator, she could only pray it was full and in good condition. When was the last time Aunt Ruth had visited the cabin?

She joined John in a long line at the cashier. The carts all looked the same. If so many people were preparing, a storm must be inevitable. She sighed. One more thing on her long list of things to make bringing Ben to justice more difficult.

Back outside, they loaded her's and John's supplies into the back of his truck. The sedan was nowhere to be seen. Lacey met John's gaze over the truck bed, his blue eyes sending electric shockwaves through her. She ripped her gaze away. Handsome or not, she had no time to explore a relationship with him. Not that he would want a relationship with her. Not after she almost killed him.

They made the drive home in silence and without the dark sedan following. John pulled in front of her dark house.

"I left a light on," Lacey said.

"Stay here." John pulled a gun from the glove compartment and exited the truck.

No way was Lacey staying behind. She had a weapon, too. Hopefully, a possible intruder wouldn't have to find out it was empty. She sprinted to his side.

John rolled his eyes and shook his head. "At least get behind me, then."

Lacey handed him the key to the front door. They stepped into silence. She reached over to flick the light switch. Nothing happened. "Do you think the electricity is shut off?" she whispered. "I didn't think to call ahead and see whether a payment needed to be made."

"Most likely. Stay close and we'll head out back to check the generator."

She nodded and stayed close enough to smell the soap he'd showered with that morning. She no longer thought someone had broken into her home, but she wasn't taking any chances.

The generator was empty. A quick call to the electric company informed Lacey service wouldn't be up and running for three to four days. She glanced out the window at the darkening clouds. She'd be a bit cold for the next few days.

"Pack what you need." John leaned against the kitchen counter. "I've a guest room you can stay in."

"The fireplace will be fine. I can't impose." She tried not to see the way his muscles strained the sleeves of his flannel shirt or the way a lock of dark hair fell across one eye. Staying under the same roof with Mr. Outdoor GQ was not a good idea. She didn't need the distraction.

"If you don't come with me, I'll alert the authorities that you are staying here without electricity or running water. They'll make you leave until the power is back on. Would you rather stay at my house or in a motel, alone, with whoever is following you maybe a door or two away?"

Good question. "I'll get my things."

~

John ushered Lacey into his home. "This is my nanny and housekeeper, Susan. You've already met my niece Meagan." He glanced at Susan. "Miss Baxter will be staying with us until her power is on."

Susan scowled. John shook his head and chose to ignore her. He didn't know Lacey well, but he doubted she would make Susan's job any more difficult. She seemed like the do-it-herself type.

"It's nice to meet you." Lacey's smile faded under the other woman's glowering look.

"I'll show you to your room." John couldn't understand why his brother had hired such a sour woman. Perhaps, it was time to find another nanny for Meagan.

He led Lacey to the only empty room in the house. A blue and white quilt covered a four-poster bed. A rocking chair sat next to a window. Other than an armoire and a nightstand, the room held little else. The hundred year old house had very few closets. Glancing at the suitcase in his hand, he doubted Lacey would need anything more.

"This is wonderful, thank you." She set a box of

things on the bed. "Thank you for letting me impose."

"Under duress, you mean," he said smiling. "Don't forget I threatened to tattle on you."

She giggled, the sound as pretty as the trickle of a brook, and pleasant to his ears. "Yes, I remember that. I think I'll be quite warm here." She removed a small chest from the box and set it on the nightstand, then placed a manila envelope next to it.

Curiosity piqued his interest. The chest didn't look like the type a woman would keep her jewelry in. Instead, it looked like a smaller version of a pirate's chest.

She caught him staring and raised an eyebrow. "Let me unpack, and I'll join you in the living room."

He nodded and backed from the room, closing the door. She was welcome to her secrets as long as they didn't affect him or his niece. The power would be on at her place in a few days, and she could go about her business.

Susan thrust Meagan into his arms the moment he entered the kitchen. "I'll need to rethink dinner, now that there's another mouth to feed. I was planning on grilled cheese and tomato soup."

"Again?" He cradled Meagan close.

"I never claimed to be a cook." She banged a pan onto the stove. "I'm here to watch the baby and clean the house."

"I'll cook." Lacey stepped up behind John. "I love cooking, and I'm good."

"Problem solved." John grinned as Susan stormed out of the room. "I don't think my brother hired her for her personality."

Lacey opened the freezer. "I'll keep my comments

to myself. How does pork chops sound?"

Real meat? He hadn't had that since arriving at his brother's place. "Wonderful." After putting Meagan in her highchair, he perched on a stool at the kitchen island. He opened a box of Cheerios and tossed a handful on the tray. Meagan gave him a smile that melted his heart.

"You're good with her," Lacey said, scrambling an egg into some milk. "How long are you watching her?"

Pain, still raw and as fresh as the day he got the call, ripped through John. He twirled the salt shaker in his hands. "As long as she needs me. Her parents are dead."

"I'm so sorry." Lacey froze, a pork chop dipped half in the egg mixture.

John shrugged. "I was her only living relative." He glanced at his towheaded niece. "She'll never know her parents."

"Sure, she will. You'll keep them alive for her." She returned to fixing supper.

Could he do that? He glanced at Meagan happily shoving cereal into her mouth. Would pictures and stories be enough to keep their memories alive for her? He truly hoped so. With God's help, he would do all in his power to make sure she knew her parents.

"I saw the makings of a salad in the refrigerator." Lacey pulled his attention back to her. "Would you mind?"

"Not at all." He slid from the stool and gathered the necessary ingredients. "Anything else?"

She shook her head. "Until I have time to see what you have, it's the pork and salad tonight."

"I'll give Meagan one of the toddler meals in the

pantry." He set to work chopping vegetables.

The hominess of the two of them working together in the kitchen, Meagan babbling from her highchair, wasn't lost on him. While he enjoyed having another adult to talk to, Susan didn't count, he didn't want to allow himself to get too close to Lacey. She would be heading to wherever she came from, and he would return to California with Meagan in a few months. Still, it didn't hurt to have a friend for even a short time.

He glanced up to see Lacey wipe a tear from her eye. "Are you okay?"

She turned red-rimmed eyes on him. "I'm in Oak Grove to find my aunt's killer. How does that make me okay?"

He stopped chopping. First, the news that her brake lines had been cut, now this. Lacey may not have brought the danger to Oak Grove, but she was going to be responsible for keeping it in their sleepy town.

"I will understand if you tell me to leave."

"No, but there is something we need to talk about." He set down his knife. "My brother and his wife died in a car accident. Their brake lines were cut, same as yours. It seems we might have a common goal."

CHAPTER FIVE

Ben Harper threw a framed photo against the wall of his deceased wife's father's house. The glass shattered, raining to the hardwood floors like shards of ice crystals. Where was the incriminating evidence?

Had that meddling niece of hers found it already? He turned around, his gaze scanning every inch of the office. The only thing that seemed to be missing was a box. At least that was the shape left on the dust-covered surface. Maybe the evidence wasn't here. No one but a fool would leave something so valuable in plain sight. He dug in his pocket for a lighter. Old man Baxter had been nobody's fool.

He'd burn the place down. If Lacey didn't have the evidence in hand, she would never find it. He lit a corner of the forest green curtains hanging at the window. If she had found it, he would know soon enough and would take more extreme measures to prevent her from doing anything with what she found.

Once the heat in the room got too intense, he

headed outside and around the corner to the outside door that led to the basement. A quick look in there, and he would head back to his hotel room to formulate his next plan.

The basement was dark and full of boxes. Ben grinned. This would be where Ruth would have hidden the box. No matter. Already smoke drifted through the floorboards and began to fill the space.

Lacey hadn't had time to scour the basement. Not the spoiled girl Ruth had raised. Oh, no. She would have taken one look at the dark, eery place and scampered back upstairs like the mouse she was. Well, Ben was going to set a trap for the little mouse. He couldn't wait, and he was going to have a bit of fun before he killed her.

~

"Why would the same man who killed my aunt want to kill your brother?" Lacey shook her head. It didn't make any sense. Should she tell him about the locked chest? She studied his strong profile.

John Canyon seemed like one of the good guys. He was an officer of the law. Was he determined to avenge his brother's death as she was her aunt's?

"I found some photos in my aunt's attic." She might as well toss the cards in the air and see where they landed. If John reacted in a matter opposite of what she wanted, or if she felt in danger, she would flee. "They were surveillance photos of her everyday life. There were a couple of me." She gripped her hands together. "I also found a locked chest. I haven't had a chance to look at it yet, not with preparing for the storm."

"Do you mind if I open it with you?" He cut her a sideways glance. "Between the two of us, maybe we'll find a clue to this madness."

"As long as I have final say in what we do with the information."

"Of course." He looked surprised.

"Well, you are a DEA agent. You might want to turn any evidence over to the police. I'm not sure I will want to do that, at least not right away." Not until she knew who she could trust.

He stopped preparing the salad and put a hand over her clasped ones. "I'm on a leave of absence. If it's true that someone is after both of our families, then we make the decisions together. You can trust me."

She stared at his strong hand over hers and hoped he was being truthful. It would be so wonderful not to have to prove Ben's guilt alone, but having a man such as John at her side sent her emotions spiraling. She didn't need the distraction.

What about the child? Things could get dangerous. John needed to think about his niece. If Lacey's staying with them put the poor little thing in danger, she would have to leave. She stared out the kitchen window as the first snow flurries began to fall.

John squeezed her hands, then returned to the salad preparations. "We'll do this, Lacey."

If he only knew how cruel Ben could be. She'd seen the bruises on her aunt's body in the morgue. Some of them had been too old to have been caused by her deadly fall. John hadn't seen the evil in her uncle's eyes when he looked at Lacey.

The pork chops sizzled in the hot oil, pulling her attention back to where it belonged. "We'll open the chest after supper."

"There's a fire outside." Susan poked her head into

the kitchen. "I think it's your place," she said to Lacey.

Lacey yanked the pan off the hot burner and dashed for the front door. She grabbed her coat off the rack and rushed outside.

"Watch Meagan," John told Susan, running after Lacey.

It was grandpa's house. The orange glow filled the sky. With tears freezing on her face, Lacey sprinted down the road.

"Wait." John caught up with her and grabbed her arm. "You don't know what you're running into."

"That house is one of the most important places in the world to me." She yanked free and continued her mad dash.

She skid into the yard, losing her footing on the sleet-covered grass and fell to her knees. It was gone. The entire place was up in flames. Grandpa's books, his antiques, everything was gone.

Her tears blurred the sight. The heat of the flames stung her cheeks.

John lifted her into his arms and moved her to a safer distance. "I'm so sorry."

"He did this." She cried into his chest, relishing in the comfort he provided. "He doesn't know I have the chest. He did all this for nothing."

"No, it's a warning." He set her on her feet, tilting her face to his. "Whether you had found the chest or not, he would have set the fire. This man is out to hurt you, one way or the other. It's personal. Why?"

She leaned her forehead against his chest. "I rejected him. After my aunt died, he made a proposition that he would take care of me. I told him no and slapped him. Suspecting he killed my aunt for her money isn't enough for him. He wants personal vengeance."

~

John had seen plenty of evil in his career. Lacey's uncle wasn't a threat he hadn't dealt with before. He glanced toward his own place. But, did he want that kind of evil anywhere close to his niece?

He looked at the woman crying in front of him. He couldn't send her away. They would have to deal with whatever came together, and pray they all remained safe. "Let's go home." He held out his hand.

"I don't have a home." She disregarded his hand and stomped past him. "All I have is a tiny place in the city that holds my things."

His heart ached for her, but standing in the open, the late, cloudy afternoon illuminated by the fire, left him uneasy. Snow continued to fall, melting instantly when landing on the flaming frame of the house. He scanned the tree line. Whoever started the fire could be watching. The hair rose on the back of his neck.

He grabbed Lacey's arm. "We have to go."

A shot rang out as they turned. Lacey stumbled. John sprinted for the opposite stand of trees, dragging Lacey with him. Once they were behind cover, he swung her to face him. "Are you hit?"

"Something ripped at my arm." She showed him a gash in the thick coat she wore. "There's no blood. I'm fine."

Relief flooded through him strongly, he almost sagged to his knees. "Run for the house. Don't stop. Don't look back."

She nodded and ran. Another bullet kicked up the snow at her feet. She screamed and swerved.

Since it seemed as if the shooter was aiming for Lacey, John kept himself between her and the trees behind them. Fear for Meagan if something should happen to him kept him running. He could stop and return fire with the gun in his waistband, but in doing so, he would put them in more danger.

He grabbed Lacey and tossed her in the ditch beside the road. "Go through the culvert. Out the other side and make for the house. It will give you some cover."

She scrambled through the cement tunnel. They splashed through the frigid water, emerging within sight of the house.

"I think … that … confirms something," Lacey said as they burst through the front door. "I'm the target."

"I agree." John latched the door and moved to close the curtains. "Susan!"

"Yeah?" She entered the living room, Meagan on her hip.

"Put Meagan down and make sure the doors and windows are locked."

"What's going on?" She frowned.

"Do as I ask, please." Why did she question everything he said?

"She'll have to be told." Lacey pulled the curtains in the dining room closed. "She needs to be given the opportunity to leave. She should leave."

John caught Susan watching from the kitchen. The smirk on her face left his blood cold. Instead of being frightened of their situation, she seemed amused. He no longer trusted her. If she didn't leave now, she could possibly be snowed in with them.

"Susan, you're dismissed. Go home. We're going to be snowbound. There's no reason for you to be stuck here with us."

"I don't mind." Her eyes widened and her smile faded.

"I won't need you. Not with Lacey here."

She cocked her head. "You'll need a chaperone, Mr. Canyon. Whatever will the women at church say?"

Three long strides brought him face-to-face with her. "Who are you?"

She stepped back. "I don't know what you mean."

"You were here before I was. I thought maybe Jason and Michelle had hired you, but that isn't true, is it?" He continued to advance until her back was against the counter. "You seized an opportunity to keep an eye on me, didn't you?"

"I saw an opportunity for a job." She crossed her arms and lifted her chin.

"Leave now or I will run you off at gunpoint." He pointed at the door.

She shrugged. "Fine, but don't blame me if rumors are started about you living out here with that woman." She shoved past an open mouthed Lacey.

Once John heard the sound of a car engine, he turned. "Will you watch my niece for me?"

"You're leaving me?" She paled.

"For fifteen minutes tops. If I don't leave now, I might not be able to." He put his hands on her shoulders. "Susan is right. If we are snowed in, tongues will wag. I won't have my niece subjected to that. I know of a woman who will help us."

"There is a shooter out there."

"You'll be safe. You have a gun. Head upstairs and lock the bedroom door." He laid a kiss on her cheek. "I'll be quick."

She nodded and scooped Meagan into her arms.

He hated leaving them, but he wouldn't tarnish the memory of his brother by having the people of the small country town think the worst. His mother's friend would help, he knew it, and the tough old woman wouldn't be afraid of a little danger.

He climbed behind the wheel of his truck and sped down the road, past what remained of Lacey's grandfather's house. Five minutes later, he knocked on the door of Mrs. Thompson's house.

"John!" She wrapped him in a hug. "What brings you out in this kind of weather?"

"I'm in need of a nanny and a housekeeper, not to mention a chaperone." He explained the possible danger.

Her lips thinned. "Of course, I'll come. Let me gather a few things. Grab that rifle over the fireplace and the ammo on the mantel."

"We could get snowed in."

"Nah. This will melt. We have a week or two before the really bad weather. I feel it in my bones." She pulled a suitcase from the coat closet.

"Are you sure you don't mind coming? I hate putting you in possible danger, but I had no one else to turn to." Maybe he shouldn't worry about a chaperone. It was the twenty-first century, after all. His word should be good enough for Oak Grove.

"Son, you're giving me the most excitement I've had in a very long time. I wouldn't miss it for the world."

CHAPTER SIX

Lacey opened the door for John and a much older woman who looked frail enough to be blown away by a strong wind. The automatic rifle slung over her shoulder dispelled the first impression.

"This is Alice Thompson," John said, setting down a large box. "She'll be staying here a while."

"Call me Alice." She met Lacey's stare and smiled. "Don't worry about the guns, sweetie. I know how to use them and use them well. I was a rancher's daughter and then a rancher's wife. I've had to run off scoundrels of the four-legged and two-legged kind. I smell supper."

She unpacked another rifle and boxes of ammunition. "I've brought some clothes and food, too. Don't want to impose."

John laughed. "You're here as a favor to me."

She patted his cheek. "And to your dear mama."

"I'll finish cooking." Lacey hurried to the kitchen, bracing her hands on the countertop.

The new nanny looked like she was prepared for a war. It wouldn't come to that, would it? A few gunshots at a burning house wouldn't result in the exchange of more gunfire, surely. It was a warning, right?

She struggled to get her breathing under control. She should keep running until she had what she needed to face Ben. Then, she would face him alone, without endangering anyone else. She glanced to the corner of the kitchen where Meagan played with blocks. If something were to happen to the little girl, Lacey would never forgive herself.

She set the pan of pork chops back on the burner and turned up the heat. Since Susan had left, Alice would have her share, or Lacey's. She doubted she'd be able to swallow a bite.

"What's wrong?" John stepped next to her, his proximity sending her pulse racing and doing nothing for her already rapid breathing.

"It looks as if we're preparing for war." She set a lid over the simmering chops.

"We need to protect ourselves. You were shot at today." He brushed her hair away from her face. "I'm calling the police."

"Wait until we've eaten. The meat has sat out long enough." She stepped away from his touch. She couldn't allow her emotions to be scrambled by the handsome DEA agent. "Then, we'll look through the chest. We'll have to decide whether to turn over whatever we find or not."

"We can't wait too long to call."

"I know." She shook her head. "Sorry. I don't mean to be snappish, but the stress is getting to me."

He pulled her into his arms, cradling her head under

his chin. "I won't let anything happen to you."

If only that was a promise he could keep. "I need to finish cooking. You must be starved." She pulled free and, avoiding his gaze, focused on mixing the vegetables he'd chopped earlier into the lettuce.

"Lacey ..."

"Later, John, please." She turned her head to hide her tears. The events of the last week was catching up with her. Somehow, she needed to find a way to keep from exploding.

She glanced up as John lifted Meagan into his arms and left the room. He cast one last look at Lacey and gave her a sad smile. The moment he left her sight, the tears she'd been holding in poured down her face.

"Well, I came in here to help you fix supper," Alice said, "but I can tell you might need more help than that. What's troubling you, sweetie?"

Lacey waved her hand. "All of this." She proceeded to pour out to the woman all that had transpired over the last week.

"Sit." Alice pointed to a kitchen stool. "I'll finish this." She grabbed a spatula and turned the chops, then pointed the utensil at Lacey. "You have to buck up. Now is not the time to fall apart. That will come later."

Lacey sniffed and wiped her face on a kitchen towel. "I know. I couldn't help it. The tears are a release."

"You're afraid, and rightly so, if all that you and John have told me is true."

"Then, why did you come? Aren't you scared?"

"I'd do anything for Annie's boy. He's helped me out more times than I can count, him and his brother. Since my husband died, I've needed something to keep me going. This will do it." She grinned, wrinkles spreading across her face like lines on a map. "I love a good fight."

Lacey smiled despite the fear racing through her. "Let's eat, then I've some evidence to make sense of." She trusted John, so if he trusted the feisty Alice, then Lacey would, too.

After they ate and she and Alice cleaned the dishes, while John put Meagan to bed, Lacey set the manila envelope and the locked chest in the center of the table. She took the small gold key from her pocket and unlocked the chest while Alice glanced at the photos.

Inside the chest was a newspaper article dated 1929 and some more photos. The article stated that a man had been hung by local moonshiners and the authorities were on the lookout for the men responsible. The only name Lacey recognized was Harper; one of the men responsible for the hanging.

She sat back in her chair. "My uncle's ancestors murdered an innocent man."

"That might be enough of a motive for him to want this info hidden," John said, reaching for the photos. "Especially if reputation means anything to him."

"It means everything to him."

~

"This looks like the barrel of a gun." John tossed a photo on the table. "And, a very large crop of marijuana in a huge greenhouse."

Lacey gasped. "You think Ben Harper has moved from moonshine to growing pot?"

He shrugged. "It's a good guess, and that is one of the largest crops I've ever seen."

"Where would someone hide a greenhouse of that

size?" Alice glanced out the window. "There's nothing farther up the mountain except government land."

John stood and paced the kitchen. It had been a long time since he'd wandered the mountain as a young boy. "If the greenhouse is disguised, they might get away with it. It has to be somewhere remote. I'm calling the authorities." He pulled his cell phone from his pocket and punched in the numbers to the two-man police department.

"Officer Harris, here."

"This is DEA Agent John Canyon." He continued his pacing.

"What can I do for you, Agent?" The rattle of paper came across the line."

"I have reason to believe you have a large marijuana crop growing somewhere on the mountain."

"Really?" The creak of a chair. "We've never had trouble of that kind here."

"I have some photos—"

"Is there any identifying things in the photos that would lead you to guess that the farm is in our jurisdiction?"

"It's a gut feeling—"

"You're basing this on a feeling? Look, Agent, you're on a leave of absence, last I heard. Get your brother's affairs in order and leave the crime solving to us."

"Don't you want to look at the photos?" John's gut feelings had never been wrong before.

"Not unless you have other grounds to warrant an investigation."

"How about the fact my neighbor was shot at earlier this evening and her house burned to the ground?" He gritted his teeth. He'd heard of the sometimes laziness of small town cops, but this took the prize.

"That warrants investigation. I'll be there in twenty minutes, longer if the snow has affected the roads." Click.

John turned to the window. "He doesn't believe us."

Lacey shoved some of the items in the manila folder. "We'll show him the drug pictures, but nothing else until we determine whether we can trust him." She rushed from the room.

"He's going to want to know why someone shot at her," Alice said. "I'm not sure this one photo is going to be very convincing."

"I agree." He sat back at the table, drumming his fingers on the Formica top. "He will ask where she got the picture."

"That's easy." Lacey leaned against the doorframe. "It was in my deceased aunt's belongings. My step-uncle is a very influential man in these parts. No one knows anything until we know, without a doubt, that we can trust them."

"I work for the law, Lacey. We need to involve them." John shook his head. "Not everyone will be in your uncle's pockets."

She hung her head, her blond hair falling across her face like liquid fire. "You said we would do this my way. I want my uncle to pay for killing the only family I had left."

He met Alice's glance, and shrugged. Until they knew the type of man Officer Harris was, he wanted to play things close to the chest, too. But, they needed to be prepared to ask for help if the man seemed honest.

A knock sounded at the door. Lacey took her seat at

the table as John answered the door. One of the largest men he'd ever seen stood on the porch, brushing snow off his massive shoulders. His gut hung over his belt. He peered at John with dark, narrowed eyes.

"You must be John Canyon."

"Officer Harris. Come in, please."

Harris stomped the snow from his boots and brushed past John, heading for the kitchen. "I wouldn't be opposed to coffee," he said, his voice booming through the room. "It's colder than a monkey's brass—" He clamped his mouth shut. "My apologies, ladies."

Alice raised her eyebrows and headed to the stove. "I'll have it ready in five minutes. We don't usually drink caffeine this late at night."

"You're old man Thompson's widow, right?" The kitchen dinette chair groaned as Harris lowered his bulk onto it. "The town hasn't seen much of you."

"I stay to myself. I have everything I need on the farm." She measured grounds into the coffee filter.

John slid the marijuana photo across the table. "This is what we have."

Harris glanced at it, without picking it up. "I'm not here about that. We don't have any proof that is anywhere near here. I'm curious about the shooting." He peered at Lacey. "You're new here. You the one that was shot at?"

She nodded. "I came to settle my grandfather's place. Someone shot at me and burned the house down."

"Now, why would someone do that? You got enemies?"

"No." Her look dared John to say otherwise.

He sighed and kept his mouth shut.

Alice plopped a mug in front of Harris. "She's Ben Harper's niece, by marriage. What fool would take the chance of making that man mad?"

"Ben Harper?" Harris paled. "Then, it must have been a case of mistaken identity. Some drunken hunters, maybe. I'll take a look around in the morning. See what I can find."

"What difference does it make who my uncle is?" Lacey slapped her hands on the table. "Someone shot at me. Deers don't wear turquoise coats. I stood out like a beacon."

"Drunk is drunk. We got a lot of good old boys who haven't a lick of sense." He sipped his coffee, staring at her over the rim. "I'll also have a talk with Ben. We're friends from way back."

If Harris was friends with Harper, then Lacey was right. There would be no trusting the overweight small town cop. Unless Lacey was incorrect in her suspicions, which she doubted. Leave of absence or not, John needed to take a closer look at her allegations.

Sometimes, even a beautiful face hid lies and deception.

CHAPTER SEVEN

The next morning, Lacey leaned on the fence and watched the two horses paw at the snow in their search for dried grass. She'd mended the tear in her coat the best she could, but the uneven stitching only served as a reminder that she had information Ben would kill for. She sighed and rested her chin on her folded arms.

She should leave. Staying would only endanger those in the house. Could she bring Ben down on her own? What did she know about the growing of illegal drugs? She couldn't go to the local police. She'd known that the moment Officer Harris stated he and Ben were friends.

Footsteps crunching on the thin layer of ice over the snow alerted Lacey that she had company. Without turning her head, she knew John was joining her. Every time the man was anywhere near, her nerves twanged, tuning into his presence. Another reason for her to leave. She didn't need the complication of a handsome man. Not only was he good to look at, but he loved his niece as if she was his own, had taken in a stranger, one that almost killed him, and hired a gun-toting nanny to help them fight the bad guys. John Canyon was danger of a different kind.

"Alice said you haven't unpacked." John propped a foot on the lowest rail.

"Why was she in my room?" Not that it was really her room, but a girl was entitled to some privacy. She lifted her head.

"She's also hired to clean." He tilted his head, studying her face. "You're planning on leaving, aren't you?"

"Don't you think it's for the best?" She turned, leaning her back against the fence. "I've brought trouble with me. Think of Meagan."

"You'll never make it out there on your own." He ran his hands roughly through his hair. "I am thinking of my niece. That's why I brought Alice here. The moment I looked at those photos and called Harris, I put myself in the line of fire. It's my job to shut down illegal drug operations."

"Not right now, it isn't. You're on leave. Pack up Meagan and go on a vacation somewhere warm." She laid a hand on his arm. "Leave this behind."

"I don't trust Harris to get anything done. This is Meagan's home. She's lost her parents, I can't take that away from her, too. Not yet."

A shadow passed over his blue eyes, wrenching Lacey's heart. She had brought him this pain.

"Stay, Lacey. Let me help you." He put his hand over hers and pulled her close. "We can't let men like Ben walk free. I grew up here. I love this community.

Help me help them. With the evidence you have, we can draw Ben out into the open and expose him."

She opened her mouth to speak, then closed it. How could she refuse? She came here to avenge her aunt. Having John's help would be better than going it alone and possibly dying before she accomplished what she set out to do.

"You can't do this for revenge," he said, brushing the back of his thumb down her cheek.

She pulled back. "How can you say that after your brother's death? My accident and his could be related. Ben might be the man responsible. Don't you want to see him pay?"

"Very much, but I want to be driven by justice, not revenge." His hand fell to his side.

"Call it what you want, it's all the same." She marched into the house and to her room.

She eyed the small chest on her nightstand, wishing she knew the area better. If she did, she'd go looking for the marijuana farm and bring the whole operation down around Ben's ears. Aunt Ruth didn't deserve for her killer to go free.

She eyed the phone and thought about calling Ben, telling him about the photos of him with another woman, and agreeing to meet him somewhere. But, John would never go for it. She grinned. Why call Ben when the mayor would be so much better?

A knock sounded on her door. "Lacey?"

Sighing, she kicked off the bed and called for John to come in.

~

"That gal has photos of the pot farm."

Ben clenched his fist. "Anything incriminating

about them?"

"You can't tell where it is or who they belong to."

"Did she show you any more photos? Any with people in them?" If she had the ones of Ben entertaining a lady of the evening, his brother would have his head.

"Not that I saw. I think we're good. I'll pretend to take a look around."

"I don't pay you to think."

"She also complained about someone shooting at her."

Ben frowned. He needed to hire someone who was a better shot than he was. He shouldn't have missed. His troubles could have been over. "Keep me informed." He hung up and leaned back in his chair.

This should have ended when Ruth went over the cliff. Sneaky woman had been smarter than he'd thought. Now, her nosy niece was taking over. He'd like to get his hands on her. She was a looker for sure. Have some fun, then toss her over to join her aunt.

He reached for the phone to call his brother. The mayor might yell and carry on, but he'd see that Ben still had everything under control.

"Mayor Harper's office."

He'd like an hour or two with his brother's secretary, too. The buxom redhead looked as if she belonged on a 1940s pin-up calendar. "This is Ben Harper. I'd like to speak to my brother, please."

"This is Roy."

"Hey, big brother."

Roy let loose a couple of colorful expletives before addressing Ben. "You've messed up big time now."

"There is nothing in the photos to point to us."

"Are you taking the word of that empty-headed, doughnut-eating cop? Of course the woman has more information than she's letting on. Her aunt was a smart woman. Find out what she knows and get rid of her and the evidence before we're ruined." Click.

~

John entered Lacey's room. "I'm sorry if I said something to upset you. As long as we work together, it doesn't matter if our motives are different. As an officer of the law, revenge isn't something I can indulge in."

"But, it is something I can indulge in." She rubbed the top of the wooden chest containing the photos. "What if I call the mayor, tell him I have incriminating photos of his brother, and agree to meet him and Ben? Then, you can have the cavalry waiting and apprehend them."

"That doesn't give us the proof we need that they murdered my brother." He crossed his arms.

Her lip curled. "Now, who's out for revenge?"

"No, I just want to make sure he receives justice for my brother's death. Meagan deserves to know that those who killed her parents were punished." If he were honest, he wanted them dead, but he'd taken an oath when taking the job as DEA. An oath he took seriously.

"Breakfast!" Alice called from the kitchen. "Get it while it's hot."

"Coming?" John tilted his head toward the door.

She nodded and brushed past him, the scent of flowers wafting from her hair. Would they have clicked better if they'd met under different circumstances? She was pretty enough, but sadness clouded her face and angry soured her mood. Not that he blamed her. He was certain they felt the same.

He entered the kitchen to smells of pancakes and frying bacon. He grabbed a doughy disc and cut it into bite-sized pieces before setting them on the tray of Meagan's highchair. Once she was happily shoving food into her mouth, he loaded his plate with pancakes, syrup, and five slices of bacon.

"You're really good with her," Lacey said. "It's surprising that you don't have children of your own."

"Never found the right woman." Now that he had Meagan to care for, he doubted he'd have time for romance. At least not in the near future. Still … he studied Lacey's face. She was here, under his roof. Maybe …

He shook his head. It was true that he hadn't found the right woman, but he had left out the fact that he had once had a lot of different women. He needed to focus on his orphaned niece. There wasn't time for a dalliance or anything more permanent. Besides, he'd left the loose lifestyle behind when God slapped him upside the head because one woman took his attentions too seriously and tried to commit suicide.

"You seem to be carrying on quite a serious conversation with yourself," Alice said, dribbling syrup over what was left of Meagan's pancakes. "Anything we can help you with?"

"No, thanks. Just making sense of my thoughts." He glanced up to catch Lacey staring.

She pierced him with her blue eyes, then transferred her attention to her food. "What do we do next? We can't sit here and wait for my uncle to make a move. Hopefully, that's part of your deep thinking."

The two of them really needed to have a serious conversation. "Have you heard the Proverbs verse about a steady drip being compared to a contentious woman?”

Tears sprang to her eyes. She bolted from her chair and to her room. The slam of the door shook the house.

“Smooth.” Alice shook her fork at him. “That girl is hurting and scared. Someone murdered her aunt and now they're trying to kill her. Being abrasive is a defense. Look deep. You'll find a tender heart.”

“You're right.” He sat back in his chair. “We're both grieving, and I wasn't the nicest person when she tried to run over me with her Jeep.”

“Now, that is a story I want to hear.”

He filled her in on the way he had met their houseguest, then cleared the table while Alice cleaned crumbs and syrup off Meagan. He needed a plan that would benefit both him and Lacey.

After stacking the dishes in the sink, he headed for Jason's, now John's office. He grabbed a sheet of paper from the printer and a pencil from a chipped coffee mug and made a list of what he knew and how they linked with Lacey's evidence.

“I'm sorry.”

He glanced up to see Lacey standing in the doorway.

“I acted like a child. I'm very aware of that Bible verse, and promise to do better in the future.” She turned to go.

“Wait.” John waved toward the straight-backed chair next to the desk. “I'm coming up with a plan. Maybe you want to hear it?”

~

The man watching through binoculars lowered them and pulled the collar of his coat higher on his neck. The minute it stopped snowing enough for the occupants of the house to leave, he intended to plant some listening devices inside.

If he didn't find out what the fool of a woman knew, Mr. Harper would put out a hit on him.

CHAPTER EIGHT

I would." She sat in the chair and clenched her hands in her lap.

"First, we go to the police station and talk to them face-to-face." He glanced out the window. "The snow has stopped and I have chains for my truck. If we don't have luck with the local police, then I will contact my supervisor in California for advice.

"Second, we start dropping hints around town that we know something, but we don't say what that something is. If the Harpers are as big as we think they are in this small community, something will slip."

"That could be extremely dangerous."

"That's why I've hired Alice. She'll do anything to keep Meagan safe while you and I step into the line of fire. Would you rather I did this on my own? You aren't law enforcement."

"And you're out of your jurisdiction. Short of arresting me, no one can keep me from finding out who, and why, my aunt was killed." She needed to move back to her place. It was a mistake to think a DEA agent would work with her as an equal.

"No one is going to arrest you. Unless the Oak Grove police do on some trumped up charge." He scrunched his mouth.

She hadn't thought of that. If she were behind bars, she would be at the mercy of a corrupt department and most likely killed. She had to stay with John. "I want to hire you as my bodyguard."

His eyes widened. "You don't have to pay me. We're in this together." He looked wounded. "Or at least I thought we were."

"Then, you'll treat me as an equal, not as an agent and a civilian. If you can't do that, I'll go it alone."

"And get yourself killed."

"Perhaps." She shrugged and picked at a cuticle on her thumb. She took a deep breath. "I'm sorry. Again. But, my Aunt Ruth was the only person who allowed me to make my own decisions, to have control over my own life." She stared at him. "I don't do well under someone's thumb."

"What do you do for a living?"

"I'm a photographer." She cocked her head. "It's a solitary job."

"You're around people all the time."

"But I'm behind the camera." She pointed at the paper on his desk. "What else is on your list?"

"We start actively searching for the location of the marijuana farm and evidence that the Harpers are the ones who hung the innocent man back in the twenties. Not your uncle, but his ancestors. It's enough to put a smear on their name. That alone would cause them to want to shut you up. Then, once we have the information we need, if no one takes us seriously or can be trusted, we go to the FBI."

It was a lot to take in. Lacey nodded. "It's a good plan. When are we heading to town?"

"As soon as I get the chains on my truck." He stood. "I'll meet you outside in half an hour. Make sure your gun is loaded and on your person."

If someone would have told her three months ago that Lacey Baxter, wedding and family photographer, would be toting a gun on a day-to-day basis, she would have told them they were crazy. Life had turned upside down with Aunt Ruth's death, and she wasn't sure it would ever be righted.

She followed John from the room. He turned in the direction of the front door, and she went up the stairs to her room. After loading the gun, she stuck it in the back of her waistband. The hard metal pressed against her spine. How did people wear it back there? She removed it and slid it into the large front pocket of her coat. Within easy reach and much more comfortable.

Back downstairs, she entered the kitchen. Alice was zipping Meagan into a down-filled jacket. "We need a few more supplies," Alice said. "Got your gun?"

"Yes." Her life had gotten very surreal. Almost unbelievable. A frail-looking old woman, caring for a baby, talked about guns as if they were an everyday occurrence.

"Good. I've got mine stuffed in the diaper bag." She grinned and hefted Meagan in her wiry arms. "Let's go see what kind of snakes we can flush from the bushes." With the toddler on her hip, she marched outside.

With a rush, the danger they were about to step into,

slapped her in the face and almost brought her to her knees. She sagged against the table. No amount of false bravado or sharp words could take away the tsunami of fear that washed over her. Acting tough, speaking harshly to keep people around her at bay, they would no longer work. Terror must ooze from every pore, visible to anyone looking her way.

She glanced up as John walked into the kitchen.

~

John rushed forward and caught Lacey before she fell. He lowered her into a chair and hurried to get her a glass of water. Holding it out to her, he crouched in front of her. "What happened?"

She pushed the glass away. "I thought it was all real when I suspected my aunt's death was no accident, then again when I fled my home. But to walk into a welcoming kitchen and see an older woman dressing a baby and talking about guns … it was too much. I'm fine, now."

"Are you sure?" He studied her face, noting the shadows under her eyes and the lines of weariness around her mouth. "You aren't sleeping well. Why don't you stay here, and I'll go to the station alone?"

"Absolutely not." She lunged to her feet and marched out the front door.

It was a good thing she had a spine of steel. She was going to need it.

The drive down the mountain and into the town of Oak Grove, population thirty-five hundred and growing, was silent except for the babbling of Meagan. John glanced in his rearview mirror and smiled at the sheer look of innocence on her face as Alice pretended to 'get her nose'.

"There is something I can't quite figure out," Lacey said, turning from the window to him. "The whole reason I fled my home was because of a robotic voice on my answering machine warning me to get out. I have no idea who left that message."

"One more thing for us to find out." And could, quite possibly, be the hardest. He couldn't help but wonder what other information she might not have told him.

He parked the old surburban, his truck as he liked to call her, in front of the red-brick police station. "Alice, do you mind heading to the store without us? We can walk from here."

"Let's meet at the diner in an hour," she said. "For coffee."

He slid from behind the steering wheel and she took his place, backing from the spot before he and Lacey were in the building. With his hand on the small of Lacey's back, he guided her into the building. He could almost feel her body heat through the thickness of her jacket. Ridiculous, but he couldn't help but focus on how, if he moved his hand a couple of inches down, his hand would rest on the curve of her hip.

"May I help you?" A curvy young brunette looked up from behind a desk and plastered on a smile.

"We would like to speak with an officer about an attempted murder," John said, scanning the area behind her.

To his left was a short hallway with two doors, one on each side. To his right, were two doors labeled his and hers. A small, no-nonsense police department.

"I'll get Officer Harris for you." She lifted the receiver on her phone.

"I'd prefer to speak with Sergeant Lawson." He felt Lacey's questioning gaze.

"Very well." The receptionist told the person on the other end that a couple requested to speak to him. "You may go back. It's the door on your right." Her smile never faded.

"Why didn't you want Harris?" Lacey whispered.

"He brushed us off after coming to the house. I'm a good judge of people, and I don't trust him. I haven't met Lawson yet, and this is our chance." He opened the door and ushered her through.

A big African-American man who stood at least two inches taller than John's six foot two, waved them toward a couple of green vinyl chairs. "How may I help you?"

"I'm John Canyon, and this is—"

"You called on the phone." He crossed his muscular arms over a massive chest.

"Yes, sir, and you blew me off."

"You asked me to reopen your brother's case. I don't have sufficient evidence to do that."

John removed the marijuana pictures from his pocket, thankful he'd had the foresight to make several copies of them. "Officer Harris visited the house the other night in regards to someone taking shots at Miss Baxter." The sergeant's dark eyes flicked to Lacey and back to John. "He said it was most likely a couple of drunks and he would look into it. I don't think he has any intentions of looking into anything. We also showed him these photos, and got the same nonchalant attitude."

Lawson leaned forward. "Marijuana fields? Where?"

"We don't know. We only suspect its on this mountain." John leaned back. "With Miss Baxter's brake lines being cut, her having possession of these photos, and then being shot at … I think it's worth investigating. You'll quite possibly see it relates to my brother's death. We have other evidence that we're holding onto for now."

He narrowed his eyes. "I could get a warrant."

"On what grounds?" John smiled. "No one seems to believe anything is going on."

They locked gazes for a few seconds, before Lawson nodded. "I'll look into it."

"Alone."

"Pardon me?"

"Alone. I don't trust Harris." John reached over and squeezed Lacey's hand. He couldn't pinpoint why, but he knew they could trust Lawson.

"Fine." He scooped up the photo and dropped them into a desk drawer. "I'll be in touch. Try to stay alive until then."

Still holding Lacey's hand, John led her from the precinct and outside. "He's on our side."

"What makes you so sure?"

"Gut instinct." He smiled. "And he wouldn't have cared whether we were alive or dead."

~

He watched as they left the police station. What had they told the Sergeant? Did they have more information than he thought? Surely, Lawson wouldn't take their claims seriously. They had no solid evidence. Did they?

With acid churning in his stomach, he placed a call to Ben Harper. "Canyon and your niece just paid a visit to the sergeant."

Ben cursed. "What did they tell him?"

"I don't know. The same thing they told me?"

"Harris, if you mess this up, you fat—"

"I said you could count on me." Why did his weight always enter into the conversation? When this job was done, Harris was going to walk the straight and narrow. No amount of money was worth the ridicule he had to endure.

He hung up and paced his office. From the glass window, he could see across the hall and into Lawson's office. The goody-two shoes. Harris hated squeaky clean cops. They made the rest of them look bad.

He turned and stared at the freshly-plowed street. At least he had a window facing outside. Most of the time, he kept the blinds closed on both windows, but the moment he has spotted the DEA and Baxter, he'd opened them and pretended to file while watching what went on in Lawson's office. Not only would he have to bug the house, but he'd have to bug the sergeant's office, too.

Grabbing a small box from his desk, he rushed to his Jeep and sped up the mountain. He could have the devices planted and be gone before anyone got a clue. He'd find out just what they knew and maybe, just maybe, he wouldn't go to Harper. Not until the man promised him more cash.

CHAPTER NINE

Lacey slid into the red vinyl booth across from Alice. She hadn't minded John taking charge in Sergeant Lawson's office, but she had minded feeling as if she weren't there.

John sat beside her, then leaned over the table to ruffle his niece's hair. "Is everyone hungry?" He glanced at Lacey. "What's wrong?"

"Nothing."

"Uh-oh," Alice said. "When a woman says nothing, she means something."

The waitress, a thirty-something woman dressed like a waitress from the fifties, with a name tag that said Barb, approached their table and pulled a pencil from her teased hair. "What can I get y'all to drink?"

"What are you going to do with the info on Harper?" John asked, pretending to look at the menu. "Sweet tea for me." He handed Barb the menu.

"What? Oh. I haven't decided yet." He needed to give her a little warning when he started dropping hints to strangers. "I'll take the tea, too."

"Tea all around." Alice grinned. "I think you should go to the person over his head. Make a real stink about the whole situation."

Lacey glanced into the face of the frozen waitress. "We aren't ready to order yet."

"Yes, fine." Her smile returned and she rushed into the kitchen.

"Sorry to spring that on you," John said, "but I recall Jason telling me something about a Barb being on the mayor's campaign committee. I took a chance you'd catch on and you did. Both of you." He grinned.

"You think she'll run straight to him with the news we have information?" Lacey pulled a napkin from the holder and tore it into a pile of snowy white. "We checked off number one on the plan and working on number two. I have to admit the thought is terrifying."

"But necessary." John placed his hand over hers to still her nervous tearing. "Tea's coming. We can't let on that we're scared, nervous … anything but confident. Harper will feed off that like a shark after chum."

Lacey shuddered at the analogy and swept the napkin pieces into her hand, then shoved them into her pocket as Barb set a large glass of iced tea in front of her. She glanced up and forced a smile to her lips. "Thank you. I think we're ready to order now. I'll have the cheeseburger meal with grilled mushroom and bacon."

"Sounds good," John said. "Make that two."

"I'll have the chicken salad with an order of fries on the side." She clipped a bib around Meagan's throat. "Little girl loves fries."

"How do you know that?" John asked.

"Because she's a female."

Lacey laughed. The woman's reasoning was probably more along the lines of she wanted the fries, and since she'd ordered a salad, didn't want to openly steer away from her healthier food. But, the fries would be easy for a toddler to eat.

She glanced out the window. Scattered snowflakes fluttered from the sky. From the look of the clouds, they weren't in for anything heavy, thankfully. The other time she'd driven on slippery roads hadn't gone well. She cut a sideways look at John.

Except, she wouldn't have met him and would have to fight her uncle alone. That would most likely have gotten her killed by now.

Speaking of getting killed. She spotted Uncle Ben, shoulders hunched against the cold, marching down the sidewalk across the street. She straightened, using the portion of wall to hide her, instead of being visible in the large diner window.

"He hasn't seen you," John said. "But, it wouldn't matter if he did. He can't harm you in broad daylight in a crowded diner."

"Do you miss anything?" Lacey relaxed, but still kept most of her body out of sight. It wouldn't be hard for someone to shoot her through the glass and be gone before anyone knew what happened.

"I'm trained to observe my surroundings. You need to learn how. Let's start with something small." He glanced around the diner. "What color are our waitress's eyes?"

"Blue?"

"Nope. Don't make easy guesses. Her eyes are

hazel. Hair color?"

"Blond."

"Height?"

Lacey thought for a minute. She was five foot four, and Barb looked a few inches taller. "I'm going with five foot six."

He grinned. "Very good. Let's do something harder." He sat back as Barb set their plates in front of them. "How many pickles are on my plate?"

"Not fair. I haven't had a chance to look at your plate." She glanced at her own and counted three. "Three."

"Nice. You didn't see, but you looked at something the same and made a reasonable deduction." He popped a french fry in his mouth.

They continued along the same vein, getting silly at times when Alice joined in. Lacey hadn't enjoyed herself so much in a very long time.

~

Ben shivered against the dropping temperatures, wishing he had the nerve to go into the diner for a cup of hot coffee. But, *she* was there.

So what? She didn't own the diner or the town, and he needed something to warm him up before his meeting with his brother.

He changed direction and jogged across the street, barreling through the door of the diner and bringing a blast of cold air with him. Ignoring the booth where Lacey sat, he climbed on a swivel bar stool and ordered a cup of coffee while ogling Barb's backside.

"Put your eyes where they belong." Barb poured his coffee, giving him a stellar view of her ample chest. "I heard something you might be interested in."

"Yeah?" He transferred his attention to her face. Not as interesting as the rest of her.

She motioned her head to the booth where Lacey and the DEA sat. "They were talking about some information they have on your brother. Said they were going to take it to someone over his head."

Ben's hand shook as his blood pressure rose. What could they possibly have, other than a few photos of an unidentified marijuana farm? Had Ruth somehow found out about his infidelities and passed the evidence to her niece? Would that be enough for Roy to blow his top? And who in the world is over the mayor's head?

"Thanks." He tossed two dollars on the counter and slid from the stool.

"No way." Barb planted a fist on her hip. "Information isn't cheap." She wiggled the fingers of her other hand.

"Fine." He tossed her a twenty, glared toward the booth where Lacey sat, and headed back out into the cold.

Roy was not going to be happy.

~

"Without turning around," John said. "Who entered the diner and what did they order?"

Lacey's hand stilled on its way to putting a French fry in her mouth. She glanced at Alice, whose eyes narrowed. "Uncle Ben, and he ordered … nothing. He's too cheap. He wouldn't have wanted anything more than coffee."

"I'm impressed. You used what you knew of someone and let the reactions of others guide you to a correct answer. My work is done for the day." If nothing else, their miniature training session had taken her mind off her fears and let her learn something practical. Something that might save her life.

The fact that Ben would brazenly enter the diner while they were there, showed the man had little to no fear over what Lacey's evidence could do to him. That, or he was more afraid of his brother's reaction to news than what she could do to him.

He watched as Ben headed across the street and toward the courthouse. Maybe a visit to the mayor wouldn't be a bad idea. He didn't want anyone to come out with guns blazing, but he did want them on their guard and making moves that might get them to trip themselves up.

"Alice, I'd like to leave Meagan with you all day tomorrow. Lacey and I are going to take the horses up the mountain to look for that farm."

"She'll be fine with me. I'll keep my eyes peeled for trouble. If any comes knocking, we'll barricade ourselves in the basement. You do know about the hidden room in there, don't you? Your brother found it right before his … accident."

"No." There was probably a lot of his brother's life he didn't know about. But, why would a private investigator have a hidden room? "Let's go. I want to take a look at that room."

He slid from the booth, scooped Meagan into his arms, and led the women to the Suburban. Before buckling his niece into her car seat, he scanned the parking lot for danger. Things looked clear; nothing out of the ordinary. As things moved forward and became more dangerous, trips to town with a toddler couldn't happen. He wouldn't put her in harm's way like that. In fact, there might come a time when he had to send her and Alice to an obscure location.

He glanced at the beautiful blond next to him. It might be a good idea to send her away, too. No matter how much he taught her in a short amount of time would turn her into a cop. He doubted she could even draw her weapon on someone if the occasion arose.

Still, he'd seen the most unlikely people turn into heroes when needed. He turned the key in the ignition and drove home.

While Alice put Meagan down for a nap, and Lacey went to her room, John flipped on the cellar light and descended the stairs. It would be easier for Alice to show him the secret room, but if it was hard for him to find, it would be just as difficult for others.

It had to be somewhere a person could duck into quickly. He ruled out behind shelves and the washing machine. The other walls had little free space as well. It seemed as if Jason and Michelle had kept almost everything that came into their house.

He ran his hand along the walls, feeling for a bump, a dent, anything that might signal a door. Frustration mounted with every step. "This is ridiculous." Maybe he should call Alice. The good thing about the search was knowing no one else would find the room easily either.

"Look down." Lacey stood halfway down the stairs.

It was in the floor? He stepped back and crossed his arms. "I can't see it."

"The light has to be just right, but the floor slightly dips." She joined him at the bottom. "But, I don't see a handle." She dropped to her knees and ran her hands over the tiles in the floor. "Ah ha!" She grinned and pressed.

An iron ring stuck above the tile. John grabbed hold and lifted a floor so precise in the placement of its tiles, that he could have looked for hours and never found it.

"Let me go first." He descended a set of wooden steps into a dirt-walled room. Hanging from a hook in the wall was a small flashlight. He clicked it on and shined it around.

Wood shelves lined the walls. On the shelves were bottles and bottles of a clear liquid. "Come on down, Lacey."

"It's for storing whiskey. She grabbed a bottle and popped the top off, wrinkling her nose at the smell wafting out.

"And I bet that if we go through the next door, we'll find the still."

"Your brother made moonshine?" Her eyes widened.

"No, but the previous owner obviously did." John opened a small door in the far wall. Sure enough, sacks of corn and sugar rotted in the corner next to a still. Even with the moonshine, it was the perfect place to hide.

"You could sell this stuff for a fortune."

He stared at Lacey, almost forgetting she was there. "Or barter with it. Do you think Officer Harris might be interested?"

CHAPTER TEN

L acey stared at the heavy bottle in her hand. While she assumed Officer Harris drank, she wasn't positive. "Do you think this moonshine is as old as the news article we found?"

John's eyes widened before he thundered up the stairs.

Lacey set the bottle on a shelf and followed. She found John bent over the kitchen table, the news article spread in front of him.

"We know the hanging took place in 1929." John glanced at the ceiling. "This house is easily a hundred years old, maybe older. What if the whiskey in the hidden room is the same stuff that got this man killed?"

"Do they give his name?" She peered around his arm at the yellowed sheets of newsprint.

"No, but I heard Jason talk about an old timer who lives high on the mountain. If anyone knows, it would be him." He folded the paper and stuck it in his pocket.

"Ready for a horse ride? I had originally planned on going tomorrow, but why wait?"

Not really. It had been years since she'd been on the back of a horse. "Sure." She forced a smile and began preparations for taking a thermos of hot coffee and cold sandwiches.

"Meet me outside when you're finished," he said. "I'll get the horses ready. Oh, and dress in layers. It's a warmer than normal day, but higher up will be cold."

She shivered. Warmer than normal? She'd thought the day freezing, despite the sunshine. Once she had their lunches prepared, she shoved them into a backpack, slipped her camera around her neck, and slid the pack on over her heavy coat. Then, on second thought, she shrugged out of the heavy coat, switched it for a lighter weight one, then carried the backpack and the heavy coat to the corral to meet up with John.

Living in a valley in the shadow of the mountain they were going to ride up, she was used to milder weather than she had experienced so far. Snow was beautiful, but it wasn't something she wanted to live with for a long period of time.

John took the supplies and hung them from his saddle. "I guess I should have asked if you could ride."

"It's been a long time." She led a mare, thick with her winter coat, to a stool. Using the stool, Lacey swung into the saddle and squirmed until she got as comfortable as possible. It promised to be a long day.

John swung into the saddle as if it was nothing. "Stay close."

As if she had plans to do anything else. He led the way behind the house and into the trees.

Determined to enjoy the ride through a forest thick

with trees, the horses' hooves muffled on the damp leaves covering the ground, she took a deep breath of the crisp winter air and kept her gaze glued to John's broad back covered by nothing more than a thin denim jacket.

"How do you know where we're going?"

"I don't." He shrugged. "I'll ride until I see smoke from a chimney, then ride up and introduce myself."

"What if it's the pot farmers?"

"I doubt they'll be cozy in a cabin. They'll want to protect their merchandise."

Good point. They were probably freezing their rear ends off standing guard.

"Besides," he added, "I do plan on checking out the place before saying howdy."

Lacey really needed to try not to appear so scared and ignorant. She really wasn't cut out for hunting down a killer. Thank God she'd run into, no, almost ran over, John. She needed someone who knew what they were doing, and they might not have met otherwise.

Her horse snorted. Its ears twitched. Lacey reined her to a stop. "John," she hissed. She pointed at the horse when he turned. "She senses something."

He slid from his horse and motioned for her to do the same, keeping his horse between him and the trees. He held a finger to his lips and removed his pistol, a Glock she thought, from its holster.

Oh, Aunt Ruth. Her death, and her stashing photos of Uncle Ben involved in dubious activities, had set Lacey on a dangerous path. She squared her shoulders and unholstered her weapon. She would see it through to the end if it killed her. Which, it might very well do. With her Magnum clenched in her fist, she hunched over behind the horse and waited for instructions from John.

He held two fingers to his eyes, then pointed across the trail before motioning for her to stay where she was. She nodded and held her breath as he ran into the bushes across from her.

How long was she supposed to wait? What if he didn't return? She couldn't visit a man she'd barely heard of alone. She peered around the horse. Would John call out if he needed help?

After what seemed like half an hour, but was more likely minutes, John returned, his weapon back in its holster. "It must have been an animal. I didn't see any signs that anyone was there."

Lacey's racing heart slowed. She also reholstered her gun and climbed, rather ungracefully, into the saddle. Already, her thigh muscles screamed and her backside burned. She'd barely be able to walk once they returned home.

The horses plodded along the trail, lulling Lacey into a semi-slumber. When John stopped and her horse veered to the side, she snapped her head up. "Are we there?"

He stared at her for a moment, his face impassive. "Are you falling asleep? I'm counting on you to keep your eyes open."

"Sorry."

He shook his head, sighed, and continued their plodding.

~

After turning back to face the trail, John released the grin he'd been holding. When he'd checked on the silent Lacey and saw her head bobbing with drowsiness, he had wanted to laugh out loud. Instead, he'd scolded her like a child. Funny and cute or not, not paying attention could get her killed.

He'd been riding toward a plume of smoke for the last hour. They'd finally gotten close enough he could smell farm animals. He stopped and slid from the saddle, then looped the reins around a low tree branch. Behind him, he could hear Lacey doing the same.

"We'll approach the house slowly and make sure it's the old man."

"Do you know what he looks like?" She stepped beside him.

"His name is Homer Snively and he's about one hundred fifty years old, according to Jason. He met him once at the diner. Said he was quite the character." Jason had also said the man was friendly. He hoped he'd heard his brother correctly. The deeper he stepped into Lacey's problems and into investigating his brother's death, the more John wondered just what it was his brother had gotten mixed up in. As a private investigator, it wasn't surprising that he saw some of the dirtier side of life, but murder and moonshine?

An old man, a rifle cradled in his arms, stepped onto the porch. "Come on out! I know you're there."

John glanced at Lacey, and shrugged. "Ready?"

She nodded.

Side-by-side, they marched across the lawn, John's gaze locked with that of the old man's. "I'm John Canyon. I believe you met my brother."

"Yep. State your business." Homer might be old, but the wiry cuss didn't blink when making a demand.

"We thought you might be able to answer some questions about a murder that took place in 1929."

"I wasn't but a kid."

"But, you heard something, didn't you?" John kept walking until the gun barrel lifted a bit. Then he held out his hand to stop Lacey.

"I reckon I might have." Homer cocked his head, then lowered his rifle. "Come on in." He entered the house, letting the rusty screen door bang shut behind him.

Putting his hand on the small of Lacey's back, John guided her inside a house as dark as a cave. Homer sat in a leather recliner which was patched so many times with duct tape it was more gray than brown. At his feet rested a copper spittoon.

"Have a seat. I see you got a thermos hanging from your saddle. I could use a cup of coffee."

John nodded, then dashed outside to retrieve the sandwiches and the coffee. It was way past lunchtime, and he was willing to give the old man one of his sandwiches for some information. When he reentered the house, Lacey perched on the edge of the faded floral sofa, laughing so hard that she clutched her stomach.

They were laughing at him, no doubt. It didn't matter. As long as she was softening up the old coot, John didn't care if they said he had three eyes. "Lunch." He set the bag and thermos on a coffee table piled high with newspapers.

Still giggling, Lacey pulled the sandwiches from the bag and handed them each one. "Do you have cups?"

"I'm not an animal," Homer said. "They're in the kitchen." Once she'd left the room, he turned his attention to John. "You're the DEA guy, right?"

"Yes, sir."

"What are you interested in an eighty-six-year-old

murder for? It had to do with moonshine, not drugs."

"I think there's a lot of different things going on here that are all connected." John took one of the cups Lacey offered and held it while she poured. He went on to tell Homer of the events of the last few days and ended with them finding the room.

He remained quiet during John's talking, then when John finished, he scratched his chin. "So, you found Boomer's stash. Clever man. I don't think anyone thought to look in his house. Making moonshine in your house is a good way to get said house blown up."

"Is this Boomer the man who was hung?"

"Yep. Old Boomer was an upstanding citizen, but on account of him being colored, some folks didn't take too kindly to him having more money than them. When he refused to stop infringing on what they thought of as their territory, some men in white sheets came calling and strung him up."

"The paper didn't say anything about him being a black man."

"Didn't want to raise too much of a ruckus when the story got out back east, I reckon. Once Boomer died, his old lady took the wife and kids back to Georgia. It's a real sad tale, so I've heard. Like I said, I was only a boy." Sandwich eaten while he talked, he now filled his bottom lip with tobacco from a tin.

John leaned forward and balanced his elbows on his thighs. "Do you know who the men were that killed Boomer?"

Homer grinned, revealing yellowed teeth. "Rumor has it that it was none other than our dear mayor's grandpa. How's that for a sordid tale?"

Combined with the illicit photos of Ben Harper with

a woman who looked like a high priced call girl, and they had the means to have the Harper family tarred and feathered. John straightened. The long ride up the mountain had been worth it.

"One more thing," he said. "Do you know the whereabouts of a marijuana farm?"

Homer laughed. "Sure I do. I have glaucoma. I'm a regular customer. Mind you, I don't buy my stuff directly from the farm, and I won't tell you who my dealer is, but I ran across the farm once."

"Are you going to tell me where it is?"

"Heck, why not? I've lived a good long life. If they find out I told, they'll put a bullet between my eyes, but it'll be quick. There was a turnoff about an hour down the trail, before you got to my place. You got to look hard, because they take caution to make the trail look untraveled, but it's there."

John met Lacey's gaze. She smiled.

They'd head up there tomorrow. They were so close to the end.

In a rare act of spontaneity, he pulled Lacey to him and kissed her.

CHAPTER ELEVEN

Lacey's eyes widened as John's kiss deepened, serenaded by Homer's cackling. She pulled back, glared from one man to the other, and dashed from the house. What was he thinking?

Who did that? What kind of man kissed a girl in the middle of a murder investigation?

She touched her lips, feeling again the strength and passion behind his kiss. In another time and place, she might relish his attentions; take the time to explore her feelings for him. But now was not that time. Not until she had avenged Aunt Ruth's death.

"I apologize."

So engrossed was she thinking of the kiss, she hadn't heard him follow. She jerked her hand from her mouth and pretended to mess with the saddle. Not that she had a clue what she was doing. She spun to face him. "Why?"

He shrugged, the corner of his mouth hitching to reveal a dimple. "I got caught up in the moment. We're getting so close. Can you feel it?" He moved closer, leading her to believe he was talking about feeling a whole lot more than how close they were coming to getting justice.

She backed up until the horse's solid body kept her from moving further. "I don't like being made a spectacle of."

"In front of who? Homer? That's probably the most excitement he's had in a long time." John crossed his arms. "I'm sorry I'm so repulsive to you."

She shivered. "It's not that." She glanced at the sky. "Looks like rain."

His expression told her he saw through her ruse to change the subject. "Yeah. We need to get off the mountain before the storm hits. We have a few hours. We'll look for the farm tomorrow."

"What about my car?"

"I'll call and check on it once I have phone reception." He swung into the saddle. "Relax. I'm not keeping you hostage."

She shrugged into her heavier coat, then climbed onto her horse. "I never said you were."

They bickered like an old married couple, both set in their ways. She ducked her head to hide a smile. It was rather humorous. After all, he'd only kissed her out of excitement. She'd retaliated by acting like a shrew. She doubted he'd ever kiss her again. For some reason, that thought left her sad.

The trip down the mountain seemed twice as long as the trip up. It was all Lacey could do not to doze off. With the stress of the past days, she hadn't been sleeping well and it was showing.

"You want to take time off from the hunt and go to

the fall carnival?" John glanced over his shoulder. "The mayor always makes a speech. Maybe we'll see something."

She shrugged. A carnival seemed frivolous, but it would put them shoulder-to-shoulder with the very people they were trying to take down.

"I've heard strange tales of the county fair," John added. "Drug dealing, prostitution, corrupt cops. We keep our eyes and ears open, there's no telling what information we'll dig up."

The temperature rose the closer they got to home. Winter wasn't arriving yet. The ice storm that pushed Lacey and John together had been nothing more than a fluke.

At the corral, she slid from the horse, shook off her heavy coat and left John to care for the horses. She lugged the backpack into the house and plopped it on the kitchen table. She glanced around for Alice and Meagan. Not finding either of them, she moved to look out the back door.

Alice rolled a ball back and forth across the grass while Meagan toddled after it. Lacey smiled. Oh, to be so innocent and unaware of the dangers that lurked around every corner. She leaned against the door frame and watched until movement in the trees caught her attention.

There it was again! She raced for the backpack on the table and grabbed her gun. Fumbling with the safety, she shoved the back door open.

"Alice, get Meagan and get in here!" Lacey aimed the gun at the trees and pulled the trigger.

~

John jerked at the sound of a gunshot. Dropping the

stall latch into place, he pulled his weapon from its holster and ran for the house. He rounded the corner in time to see Alice put Meagan in the house, then return with a shotgun.

"What is it?" He scanned the yard.

"I saw someone in the trees." Lacey pointed. "They aren't there now."

"Stay in the house." He took off in the direction she had pointed.

With the thick canopy overhead, it was hard to tell if someone had stood in the carpet of decaying leaves and pine needles. Still, John slowed and studied the ground with every step he took. There! A scud mark as someone turned quickly.

John stood where the person had. He had a perfect view of the house and back yard. He wasn't convinced that the Harpers would harm a child, but wouldn't put it past them to abduct her as a means of getting him to cooperate.

Torn between following the tracks and heading home to check on Meagan, home won out. Whoever had been watching was gone. He'd instruct Alice not to let the child play outside until this was all over.

Back at the house, he barged into the kitchen and straight to where Meagan clutched a cookie in her hand. Tear tracks marred her face.

"The gun scared her," Lacey said, looking apologetic. "I'm sorry."

"Don't be. You were looking out for us. She's fine." He wiped the tears away with his thumbs, kissed her forehead, and left Meagan to enjoy her cookie comfort. "There was someone watching. I found his tracks, but didn't follow. From now on, no outside, unless you're headed to the barn or to one of the vehicles, then make it fast. We're on high alert."

He locked the back door, then moved to the front of the house to make sure the lock was engaged on the front. Then, he checked each of the windows before rejoining the women in the kitchen.

Pulling his cell phone from his pocket, he dialed Sergeant Lawson.

"Lawson."

"This is John Canyon. We've had a trespasser."

"Are they still there?"

"No, sir, we ran him off at gunpoint."

The sergeant's heavy sigh drifted through the air waves. "Be careful with that. If you shoot someone, you'd better be sure you can back up your reason why."

"I will. Any news on what we spoke with you about?"

"I'm keeping my eye on Harris and the Harpers. Harris isn't in today. My guess … he's the one paying you a visit. He's mean and one of the dirtiest cops I've run across. The more I dig, the more I need a shower. I'd like to arrest him, but I think we need to see whether he trips himself up and leads us to those lining his pockets. Be careful. I'll let you know when I learn more." Click.

John agreed it was best to leave Harris alone for now. He wasn't the first cop on the take that John had run across.

"What next?" Lacey sat across from him, her gaze glued to his.

A man could get lost in her mixture of strength and vulnerability. "Same as before. We go to the fair tomorrow."

Alice huffed. "I suppose you want me to stay here."

John chuckled. "And miss out on fair food? No way. I want us to look as un-intimidating as possible. We'll be one big happy family."

"Sitting ducks, you mean." Lacey propped her chin in her hand.

"Whatever Harper and his hired hands might be, they aren't going to start shooting in a public place." If they did, then everything he knew as a law man, every talent he had for judging people, was wrong. "We'll be armed. Alice, you stay for a short time, then bring Meagan home. Lacey, you and I will pretend to be an item, lovers on a night off."

Her eyes widened.

He held up a hand to stop her protests. "I'm sure people are already thinking it, with you staying here. If they don't think we're an item, then questions will arise that we aren't prepared to answer."

"They think we're living in sin?"

"I'll make coffee." Alice handed Meagan a sippy cup with juice and grabbed the coffee pot.

"If they don't know Alice is living here, then yes. Does it matter? What do you care what people think, as long as the outcome is the same? We make the Harpers pay for the crimes they've committed." John rolled his head on his shoulders. "I got a text that your Jeep is ready. We'll pick it up before the fair."

She frowned, clearly not happy about them masquerading as a romantic couple. He shrugged. No matter. She'd fall in with any plan he came up with if it meant putting Ben behind bars. He grinned. There were worse things than pretending that Lacey was his main squeeze.

"What's so funny?" She glared.

"Nothing." His smile didn't fade, despite the shaking of his head. She sure was cute when she was mad. Meagan fussed and held out her arms to be held, giving him somewhere else to look other than Lacey's flashing eyes.

~

Harris leaned against a thick oak tree trunk and struggled to catch his breath. He huffed out a few expletives directed toward Harper's step-niece, then straightened, putting hands on his wide hips. He never would have guessed she would have the gumption to shoot.

Now, after running, he felt like he was going to have a heart attack, and was most likely going to get caught in the rain. He should have returned fire, taking out Harper's number one threat. Instead, he'd fled like he didn't have an ounce of courage.

Not true. He was a brave man. Only such a man could look evil in the face every day and keep going.

He pushed away from the tree and shuffled toward the road where his truck was. Why couldn't Harper have gotten himself in trouble during springtime? Fall was in full swing and the nights were as cold as a brass spittoon. He hunched over to preserve his warmth just as the first raindrops began to fall.

Cursing, he increased his speed, lumbering for the protection of his automobile. He yanked the door open as the pregnant clouds gave birth to a deluge.

His truck slipped and slid on the dirt roads as the rain turned the surface to mud. Harris wiped the moisture from his face with the back of his forearm, turned on his headlights, and did his best to peer through a windshield barely visible under the onslaught. He should have replaced the wipers months ago.

The back of the truck fishtailed, taking him sliding toward a massive pine tree. Harris screamed like a girl and wrenched the steering wheel. The truck stopped inches from the tree trunk. Shaking like an old Chihuahua, he rested his forehead on the steering wheel and took deep breaths.

That was close. He needed to drive slower. It wouldn't do anyone any good if he killed himself. He pressed the gas.

The tires spun, not able to gain traction on the wet road. Harris cursed again and pounded the steering wheel. Anger spent, he pulled his cell phone from his pocket and dialed for a tow truck.

Someone was going to pay for the day's frustrations. And he knew the perfect, lovely little blond that owed him.

CHAPTER TWELVE

They looked exactly like a family, right down to the little old grandma pushing the stroller. Except, Alice wasn't like any grandmother Lacey had ever met. And never in her wildest dreams would she have guessed she'd be in a relationship with an Alpha male like John, pretend or not.

Usually a quiet and solitary person, Lacey hadn't dated much in life, therefore, she felt inadequate in relating to the opposite sex, especially a handsome, viril man like John. She cut him a sideways glance as they approached the entrance to the fair. Still, she'd seen the occasional gleam of admiration when he looked at her. Maybe, once Ben and his friends were behind bars, she could take some time to see whether a relationship with John was possible.

John purchased their paper bracelets which allowed them to ride the rides without holding onto a fistful of tickets, and slipped Lacey's around her wrist. Her breath caught at his closeness.

Stop it! She needed to focus, pay attention to what went on around her. There were more important things than the way he smelled or how his warm breath tickled her arm as he bent over her.

"Okay," he said. "Eyes and ears open." He gave a crooked smile. "We might even squeeze in a bit of fun." He took Lacey's hand in his, causing her heart rate to accelerate. "Let's take Meagan to see the animals."

Inside the livestock shed, John perched Meagan on his shoulders and they gazed at the fattest cow Lacey had ever seen. Some prankster had stuffed a pair of denim pants and placed them where it looked as if the animal was lying on someone. A smile teased at her mouth as Meagan giggled and pointed. Lacey lifted the camera around her neck and snapped a photo not only of the cow and dummy, but of the joy on Meagan's face.

She leaned her arms on the fence around the animal and continued to watch the cow chew her cud as the others moved on. There was something relaxing about the animals. Soft moos and the clucks of chickens filled the air along with the not unpleasant scent of manure.

Maybe she should rebuild her grandfather's house and live there, along with some chickens and a goat or two. Being a photographer, she could put down roots almost anywhere.

Someone grabbed her arm and pulled her behind a horse stall. Before she could gather enough breath to scream, a hand clamped over her mouth.

Hot breath covered her neck. "We can do this easy or we can do this the hard way." Ben Harper chuckled. "Hand over whatever it was that your aunt left you, and you can go on with your sordid little life of living in sin with Mr. Canyon." His free hand groped at parts of her body better left untouched.

She gasped and squirmed against his hold.

"I like it when they struggle. Remember that next time." He shoved her hard enough to send her face first into a pile of hay.

When she struggled to her feet, he was gone. She spit hay from her mouth and crossed her arms across her middle. If he could violate her in such a way in a shed full of livestock and people, what would he do if he ever got her alone?

She couldn't let John know what had happened. Not yet. She didn't need him going after Ben before they had the evidence to put him behind bars.

"Lacey?" John called down the aisle.

"Coming." She smoothed her hair, checked her clothes for bits of hay, then stepped into the aisle, forcing a smile to her face. "Just getting a closer look."

"A real close look." He plucked hay from her hair.

"I tripped. Where to next?"

He cocked his head, then obviously decided to leave her to her secrets. "Kiddy rides? Then Alice can take Meagan home, and we'll do some investigating. We'll drive your Jeep back to my place."

"Sounds good." She led the way down the aisle and into the fall sunshine. Compared to the cold days prior, today was almost springlike. It wouldn't last. Another week or two, and they might be snowed in up on the mountain. If not snow, then ice.

"You aren't fooling him one bit," Alice said, stepping to her side. "John Canyon is an astute man. He can tell a liar from a mile away. You didn't trip in the shed, did you?"

"Sure, I did." Lacey frowned. "How could anyone attack me with people around?"

Alice narrowed her eyes. "It's best to be up-front with him at all times. He's a good man, a kind man, but lying isn't tolerated easily."

"I'm sure he'll know all he needs to know in due time." Lacey increased her pace until she was once again at John's side.

Meagan reached down from his shoulders and plucked Lacey's knit hat from her head, then tossed it. It dropped like a stone into a puddle.

"Sorry about that," John said, retrieving the beanie. "It's a game to her." He lifted the child from his shoulders, then keeping a grip on her hand, got in line for a pony ride. He glanced over his shoulder at Lacey. "You've got some blood on your lip."

She gasped and clapped a hand over her mouth.

~

John did his best to keep his composure while Meagan played and squealed on the rides. Then, avoiding Lacey's skittish glances his way, he helped Alice buckle the child into her stroller. After a kiss on the cheek, he sent his niece back home with her armed babysitter.

Taking a deep breath, he squared his shoulders and ushered Lacey behind a food vender stand. "Mind telling me what really happened in the animal shed? Don't tell me nothing. Your lip is bleeding and you have bruises forming on your face that looked a lot like finger marks." He crossed his arms to keep from forming his hands into fists.

Her eyes widened, and she touched her face with trembling fingers. "Ben grabbed me. He said if I handed over what Aunt Ruth gave me, he'd leave me alone."

"You know he's lying, right?" John would break the man's fingers. Every. Single. One, that had marred Lacey' face. "He won't leave you alone until he is either behind bars or you're dead."

"I know." She stiffened, her gaze piercing his. "So, now what? I wait for him to contact me again?"

"Pretty much." The thought made him sick to his stomach. If he could keep her from setting eyes on the man again, he would. He took her by the elbow and led her to a large tent set up as a small dining hall. "Let's grab something to eat. Once it gets dark, things really start hopping around here. If we're going to keep up the charade of a couple in love, we're going to need to eat."

She yanked free. "The *charade* was your idea. You can stop at any time."

"That's not what I meant."

"Then, what did you mean?"

"I don't know." He ran his hands through his hair. "I'm frustrated. I'm sorry. I'm scared." There. How was that for honest?

She tilted her head to one side. "Thank you. I'll take chili fries with lots of cheese." She grinned and sat at an empty table. "And a diet soda, please."

John stood in line to place their orders. He may act like a man out for an evening of fun, but his senses were on high alert now that Meagan was safely out of the way. He should have paid better attention in the animal shed. The thought of what could have happened to Lacey while he was pre-occupied soured his stomach.

Order placed, and ticket in hand, he sat at the table

across from Lacey and glanced at their number. 109. "I should ask for some ice for your face."

"Is it that bad?" She cupped her hands around her cheeks.

"Lovely shade of blue and purple showing up." He ran the back of his thumb down her face. So soft. "I'm sorry I wasn't there. I told you I would protect you."

"It happened so fast, and you were with Meagan. I shouldn't have lagged behind."

"109!" A young girl with a tray wandered between the tables calling their number.

John raised his hand.

She set the tray in front of them. Two large sodas and two plates heaping with chili fries and cheese. "Enjoy."

"I can feel my arteries hardening just looking at the food," he said.

"But, it will taste mighty fine." Lacey snagged a fry between two fingers and popped it into her mouth, closing her eyes. "Yum."

He forgot for a moment that they were trying to stay alive and bring down a drug ring. He laughed and dug into his meal. It wouldn't hurt to relax for a moment and simply enjoy Lacey's company.

A small string of cheese dangled from her bottom lip. He reached over and brushed it away, staring into eyes as deep as the mountain lake. It wouldn't take a lot of work to pretend to be interested in someone like Lacey Baxter.

"So, what exactly happens at the fair once the sun goes down?"

~

The parts of Lacey's body Ben had felt stirred his

blood like no other woman's had. Such a pity she would have to die.

He stared out his office window at the trees quickly losing their autumn foliage. He had taken a great risk approaching her at the fair. Still, his blood raced from their meeting. Maybe he was being foolhardy, but the thrill was like an addiction that drew him with the fingers of a lover.

"Are we ready for tonight?"

Ben shook his head. "Don't you ever knock, Harris?"

"You told me to be here at six. It's six." Leather creaked as he lowered his bulk into a chair.

Sighing, Ben turned to face him. "Are the trailers set up? We do a booming business every year at the fair. I don't want you messing anything up."

"We're ready to go. Got enough of a variety to suit anyone's taste." He grinned, folding his hands over his paunch. "I'm going to take me a vacation with my cut."

"You won't be going anywhere until Lacey Baxter is taken care of."

"Want that to happen tonight?" His beady eyes gleamed.

"No, not yet." Ben sat behind his desk, settling into the fine leather as if it were made for him. "I want her end to be special." He picked up a silver-plated pen and twirled it between his fingers.

"What kind of special?" Harris leaned forward and snagged a chocolate from a crystal candy dish. Unwrapping it, he popped it into his mouth as he reached for another piece.

Ben rolled his eyes at the fat man's gluttony. "Remember, no indulging in your own tastes until the end of the night. Our customers expect fresh merchandise."

Harris frowned, looking too much like a Shar Pei than any human man should. "I know."

"You're an animal." Ben waved his hand. "Get out. I'll see you later."

He watched as the policeman waddled from the room, his belly spilling over his belt. How could the city let someone like him represent their police force? It was disgusting. Once Lacey was taken care of, getting rid of Harris would be next on the list.

The phone rang, pulling him out of his thoughts. He grabbed the receiver. "Ben Harper."

"What are you doing in your office?" Roy's voice boomed over the wire. "You should be supervising the set up. Don't tell me you left things to that imbecile Harris."

"It's all taken care of."

"Remember … bring me the proceeds before you go home tonight." Click.

With a curse, Ben slammed the phone back on the receiver and grabbed his suit jacket. He might as well double check Harris's work. His brother would have his head if things weren't done to his satisfaction.

Sometimes, being the brother of a corrupt mayor was more work than it was worth.

CHAPTER THIRTEEN

The atmosphere at the fairgrounds changed with the setting sun. Families gathered up their small children and left, leaving the grounds to single men, teenagers, and lovers. The dining tent hung up a shingle advertising "specialty drinks". It didn't take a rocket scientist to know that liquor license or not, alcohol was now on the menu. Not only that, but Carnie callers barked out that every taste was satisfied if one knew where to look.

Colored lights flared to life. Music blared louder. The air vibrated with tension so thick a person would need a chainsaw to cut through it. People laughed louder. Faces glowed with expectation.

Lacey stepped closer to John. "What's going on?"

"Stay close." He grasped her hand. "Welcome to the county fair nightlife. Something you can only find in this lovely town."

Confused, she increased her pace to keep up with him as they got in line at the Ferris Wheel. "I hate this ride."

"It's the best place to view the entire grounds." He winked at her. "Don't worry. I'll keep you safe."

Maybe. She eyed the monstrosity towering above them. If someone wanted to harm them while they were trapped at the top, who would save John? She clutched his hand tighter and tried to focus on the boisterous gaiety around her.

She hadn't been to a county fair since she was a teenager herself. Things had changed. Instead of innocent joy, an undercurrent of something dirty, evil, laced the air. She shuddered.

Way too quickly it was their turn to step inside the car from hell. She scooted as far back as she could and gripped the bar in front of them so tight her knuckles hurt. She gasped and closed her eyes as the car started to rise.

"I'm sorry. You really are frightened."

She opened one eye to see John peering at her with concern. "I'm afraid of heights. Especially when I'm closed in and can't escape." She closed her eyes again.

"All right, sweetheart." He put a hand on her knee. "Keep your eyes closed. I'll do the looking."

She wasn't silly enough to believe he meant anything by the endearment or the soft touch of his hand on her knee, but she took comfort in his closeness all the same.

Once the car stopped at the top, she peeled her eyes open a slit and peered over the rim of the car. Long lines formed at every attraction, but none so long as the line of men at the back of the fairgrounds in front of plain white aluminum trailers.

Her eyes popped all he way open. "Prostitution? I

thought that every taste being satisfied was for drug preference."

"I'm sure that's for sale, too." He leaned forward, causing the chair to rock.

She shrieked and tightened her grip. "Be still."

"My brother hinted that such things were happening in Oak Grove, but without proper evidence, I wasn't able to help him." He sighed. "Now, not only have we discovered we're dealing with drugs, but prostitution as well. How could Lawson not have known?"

"Some people don't want to see." Remaining as still as possible, she turned her head. "Or, perhaps like you, he didn't feel he had sufficient evidence." She lifted her camera and snapped a few pictures of the lines in front of the trailers. "It's too far to really see what the trailers are for."

"Yeah." John nodded. "I'm going to have to go down there and pretend to be a customer."

"Won't they recognize you?"

"I'll be careful. If I'm really lucky, I'll manage to get some pictures with my cell phone."

She didn't like it. He'd be as close to the danger as possible. Where did that leave her? Hiding in the shadows trying not to be killed or abducted?

She glanced at the star-studded sky. From the top of the Ferris Wheel, she felt as if she could reach up and pluck a star from the velvety blackness.

Was God watching? Listening? Or had she stepped so far from His grace on her quest for revenge that He'd turned his face? She hoped not. She and John were going to need divine help in the days and weeks to follow.

After what seemed like an eternity, their car stopped

its rotation and let them off. John took hold of Lacey's hand again and pulled her next to the port-a-johns. "I need you to wait for me here."

She shook her head. "The dining tent. More people." And light. Lots and lots of light.

"If you're in plain sight, Ben Harper will wonder where I am. I need you to hide." He planted a quick kiss on her forehead. "If I'm not back in an hour, call Lawson." He dashed away, leaving her feeling more alone than she had ever felt before.

She stepped back and melted into the shadows.

~

John pulled a knit hat from his back pocket and tugged it over his hair. Shoving his hands into his pockets, he slouched, keeping his head down and made his way to the back of the fairgrounds.

He felt as if he needed a shower before stepping foot inside one of the trailers. He pressed record on his cell phone, and moved forward. Giggles, curses, and the smell of beer filled the inside of a metal trailer divided into small rooms. He fished a fifty dollar bill from his pocket and bought his ticket for entry.

"Enjoy!" An overly made-up woman wearing a skimpy female genie costume smiled and waved him forward. "Find the first available girl that suits your fancy. You have thirty minutes."

John forced a grin and pretended to stagger down the hall, ducking into the first available one. A young girl, she couldn't be more than sixteen, smiled up at him.

"Ready for some fun?" Her words slurred.

John pulled out his phone and took her picture, then snapped several more of the small room. "Just want the company."

"Okay, but you aren't supposed to take pictures." She scooted against the headrest.

"Do your parents know where you are?" He perched on the side of her bed.

Tears filled her eyes. "I haven't seen them for three years. Not since Mama's boyfriend hit me and I took off."

"Do you like working for the carnival?"

She laughed. "My boss calls himself a private contractor. We move around the country. Look, mister. Either you partake of what I have to offer or move on. I don't have time for do-gooders."

"I paid for thirty minutes. Want to get out of here for a few of them?" Hopefully, she wouldn't raise an alarm once they were outside, but he was going to get at least one of these girls to a safe place whether she wanted it or not. "I could buy you a drink or something to eat."

She tilted her head, as if considering his offer, then nodded. "But, if you get me in trouble, it's going to cost you."

"I'll cover any expense." He held out his hand, wincing at the skimpy negligee she wore. "Do you have a jacket or something?"

"I have a robe, Mr. Prude." She slipped a cherry red robe over the nightgown, then slipped her too skinny arms around his waist. "I want a cheeseburger. But, we'll have to hurry. They have men who keep time."

"What's your name?"

"Cherie."

He'd allowed himself to get distracted by a child in need. Slipping his hand into his pocket, he turned off the recorder on his phone and pretended to be involved in the cutie at his side. Lacey was going to kill him. But, he couldn't leave her there. He'd take them all away if he could, but would be satisfied with one for tonight.

John led the girl to where he had left Lacey. "I want you to meet someone."

"What … who?" Lacey planted her fists on her hips.

"Who is this? Your wife?" Cherie frowned. "I don't want any trouble."

"Call Lawson," John told Lacey. "I'll explain in a minute. We don't have a lot of time."

Cherie took a couple of steps away. "You really do want to save me."

"Yes, I do." He peered into her face. "Will you let me?"

"What is going on?" Lacey hissed. "Does she have something to do with Ben?"

"Something like that." John took hold of each of their arms and dragged them along the far perimeter of the fairgrounds. He stopped behind the large building used for concerts and peered around the corner. The parking lot was almost deserted. People had already arrived for their night of fun and it was too early for most of them to leave.

"To the Jeep. Quickly."

They ran, their feet sounding abnormally loud in the night. Cherie cried out, and started limping.

How could he not have noticed her bare feet? Hardly stopping in his race to the Jeep, he scooped her into his arms.

Once there, Lacey whipped open the back door. He set the girl inside and rushed for the driver's seat.

As they sped onto the highway, he filled Lacey in on his spur of the moment decision. She listened, nodding occasionally, then dug her phone from her pocket. She called Lawson, asked him to meet them at the station, then turned and took a picture of Cherie.

"I understand why you jeopardized our investigation," she said. "It was a surprise, that's all. If we can get her to give a statement, it could actually help us."

"Thank you." He placed a hand over hers. "I think so."

"You're taking me to the cops?" Cherie leaned between the two front seats. "They'll arrest me. I'll be killed."

"Sit back." John thrust out his arm. "You'll be in protective custody. I promise."

"You sure make a lot of promises." She flopped back and crossed her arms. "If I get killed, I'm haunting you."

He grinned at Lacey and increased their speed toward town.

~

"Where is she?!" Ben slammed open doors.

"A man bought thirty minutes of her time," the woman at the door said, scurrying after him. "He must have taken her out the back."

Ben whirled and backhanded her across the mouth. "What do we pay you for?" Roy was going to blow. "What man?"

"A big man. He wore a dark beanie and kept his head down."

John Canyon. It had to be.

He gripped his hair in his hands and groaned. What

did he do now? "Shut this place down. Now!"

He ran up and down the hall, banging on doors and kicking out the customers. When he'd finished with that trailer, he moved to the next, shouting orders to load up and pull out. They had to be gone before the authorities showed up. What was he going to tell Roy?

"Where's Harris?"

"Here." The man fumbled with the zipper on his pants.

Ben opened his mouth, outraged that he was playing while on the payroll, but snapped his mouth shut and doubled up his fist instead. The right handed hook he laid across the man's jaw felt good, despite the pain radiating across his knuckles.

Harris fell like a chopped tree.

"Drag him into the alley and leave him there." Ben marched outside.

People scattered like mice chased by a cat. Idiots. They couldn't look more guilty if they tried.

He pulled a Glock from inside his jacket and held it at the head of a man demanding his money back. "This is the only refund you're going to get. If you're dissatisfied, take it up with the cops. I'm not the only one breaking the law here."

The man ducked away.

Ben huffed and marched to the back lot where his Mercedes waited. This phone call needed privacy.

CHAPTER FOURTEEN

Sergeant Lawson was sliding behind the wheel of his Dodge truck when John parked behind him. The officer glanced over his shoulder and frowned before exiting the vehicle. He marched to the Jeep and peered inside. "What now?"

"We need to speak with you inside." John shoved his door open, then yanked open the one in back. "Come on." He wiggled his fingers at Cherie.

Lawson's eyes widened. "You have got to be kidding me." He shook his head, glanced around the parking lot, then motioned his head to the back of the building.

John took both Cherie's and Lacey's arm and hurried them after the officer. If they were caught now, he'd risked their plan for nothing.

"You're hurting me!" Cherie yanked free. "I said I'd come with you, and I am. No need to drag me like a sack of dead cats."

A bark of laughter escaped him. The teen had a way

with words, for sure. From the amused glance on Lacey's face as she also pulled her arm free from his grip, she agreed.

Lawson unlocked the back door to the station and waved them through. "Put the girl in the conference room next to my office. Canyon, you step into the office. Ma'am," he nodded at Lacey, "if you wouldn't mind keeping an eye on our guest …"

She didn't look pleased with the suggestion, but gave a curt nod and marched to the appointed room with Cherie. Good girl.

John needed Lawson's undivided attention. He needed the man to see the danger surrounding Oak Grove and unreservedly pool his resources with John. He glanced at Lacey as she closed the conference room door, then stepped into Lawson's office.

"Close the door. We can see the girls through the window." Lawson rolled up a set of blinds on the wall, revealing the conference room. "Mirrored window." He grinned and took his seat behind his desk. "Now, tell me what your bleeding heart has led you into now."

John explained about Lacey's assault and his acting as customer to the more lurid side of the fair. "I couldn't leave the girl there."

"No, I suppose you couldn't." He steepled his fingers, his dark eyes narrowing. "Has it once occurred to you that I may already know what goes on in this town and it suits my purpose?"

Surely, John couldn't be that far off on his character analysis. He would have sworn on his brother's grave that Lawson was an honest cop. "What possible purpose could you have for letting this go on under your nose?"

"That's classified. Especially to a DEA that is on leave." He glanced at the window between the rooms. "What am I supposed to do with her?"

"State evidence?"

"That's manpower I don't have." He sighed. "I'll send her to St. Louis to a safe house. They can protect her until this thing comes to a boil."

Cherie approached the glass and knocked, then pantomimed drinking. Obviously, it wasn't her first time in a police station.

John chuckled. "I will leave the little princess in your hands. Maybe you can find a relative decent enough to take her in when this is all over."

"You made my job that much more difficult." Lawson pushed to his feet. "I need y'all to leave before Harris gets here. Once it's discovered what you've done, he'll be here like a fat kid on a lollipop, acting all innocent and outraged. It's going to be hard enough to act like I don't have a clue what's going on."

"And the girl?"

"I'm making a call right now to have her picked up." Lawson grabbed his phone. "Go." He waved a hand. "I'll call you when I know something."

John wanted to shake the man's hand, but refrained when the officer dialed his phone. He huffed a sharp breath and hurried to the room next door.

"Sergeant Lawson is having you taken to a safe place in St. Louis," he told Cherie. "Lacey and I have to go, now."

"You're leaving me?" Cherie clutched his shirt. "You can't. I don't trust the cops. I'll be dead by morning."

"You can trust Lawson." He hoped. He prayed. The

last thing he wanted was the girl's death on his hands. He cupped her cheek. "You're better than this, Cherie. Remember that. Make something good with what's left of your life."

~

Lacey's heart ached for the frightened girl, but they couldn't take her with them. She gave Cherie a quick hug. "Sometimes, you find someone good in this life." She slipped Cherie a slip of paper with her phone number on it. "John Canyon is such a person. Call me. If I can help you, I will."

Tears ran down the girl's face, leaving tracks of mascara on her cheeks. She slipped the paper under the strap of her nightgown, looking every bit the lost little girl that she was. Before Lacey could change her mind and take the girl with them, she whirled and rushed after John.

They jumped into the Jeep and roared from the parking lot. She wasn't sure whether God listened to her anymore, but just in case, she sent a fervent prayer heavenward for Cherie's safety … and theirs.

By the time they arrived at John's house, Lacey couldn't call it home, it was almost midnight. They roared into the driveway. The porch light flickered on.

Seconds later, Alice, shotgun in hand, stepped onto the porch. "Thought I was going to have to call out the posse to hunt you two up."

"You almost had to." John put his hand on the small of Lacey's back and hurried her up the stairs and into the house.

Her back burned from his touch. If she hadn't known what a good man he was before that night, seeing his concern over a lost little girl showed her what a rare person he was. More than ever, she wanted a chance to explore a relationship with him. Someday. Maybe. If they lived long enough.

"There's coffee in the kitchen," Alice said. "Come and fill me in on what happened."

Lacey's feet dragged. Now that the adrenaline of getting Cherie to safety, and her and John returning home, exhaustion swamped her. She plopped into a chair and rested her forehead on her folded arms, wanting nothing more than to go to bed.

John ran his hand across her back as he headed for the coffee pot. "We confirmed there is more than drugs being peddled at the fair."

"And John rescued a child prostitute," Lacey said, not lifting her head. "We turned her over to Lawson."

"Too bad you couldn't shut the whole thing down." Alice slammed a mug on the table. "That racket's been here since the 60s. My dear, Frank tried to get the state police interested, but the Harpers had too many of them on the payroll."

"If we can bring down Ben and Roy, we'll take them all down." John tapped Lacey on the head.

"Just put in an IV," she said, looking up.

"Drink. You'll feel better." He filled her mug.

She doubted it, but was too tired to argue. Instead, she wrapped her hands around the hot drink and took a deep breath. "If we drink this, we won't be able to go to sleep."

"Then don't drink it." John sat across from her. "Can you go straight to bed after the adrenaline rush of the night?"

She shrugged. "Probably not." More than likely, she'd lay and stare at the ceiling until the sun made its appearance. "Now what? Harper will move the prostitution ring, at least until next year."

"I recorded my conversations and took some pics." John leaned back in his chair. "If Cherie testifies, that will be enough."

"So, now we need to prove they murdered my aunt." One way or the other, the Harpers' reign of terror was going to end. "I'm not stopping with what we discovered tonight."

"I don't want to either. I want justice for Jason just as much as you want it for your aunt. But, if it gets to the point where we're losing, where they might get away with it all if we don't bring forth what we have, then I'll put it all out on the table and step away."

He might as well have said, "Like it or not."

She lifted her head fully and met his gaze, trying to let him know without saying anything that she wouldn't be manhandled. Handsome and good or not, she wouldn't let him dictate her future. Not without discussion. If he could convince her, beyond a doubt, that his way was best, she would concede. But not until that point.

"I'm going to at least lay down and rest. If I sleep, great." She pushed to her feet. "Who knows what tomorrow holds."

"Goodnight, Lacey. I'll check in on you in a bit, if you want." John's soft words followed her down the hall.

It was getting increasingly harder to stay irritated at him. She opened her bedroom door and let her eyes adjust. Not that she expected anyone to be hiding there since Alice had been home, but she'd read somewhere it was a good idea when people were after you.

She scanned through the gloom. Nothing seemed out of place. The curtains hung still over a closed window. The closet door was shut tight. Unless someone was in there or under the bed, the coast was clear. She flicked on the light.

Feeling a bit foolish, she knelt and lifted the bedspread. Nothing. She moved to the closet and yanked open the door, rummaging through the few clothes hanging there. Again, nothing. Sighing a breath of relief, she perched on the edge of the bed.

"Satisfied?" John grinned from the doorway.

"I've hardly had time to need checking on," she said.

"I thought it wise to check the rooms. Alice said the coast was clear, but she was gone for a few hours. A patient killer could hide for that amount of time."

True. She toed off her boots. "Goodnight, John."

"Sweet dreams, Lacey." He gave her a crooked smile, then walked away with that long-legged, sexy stride he had.

She groaned and fell back on the bed.

~

Harris sat up and rubbed his jaw. Ben didn't have to hit him. He wasn't the only one working that was also indulging. One of these days, the man was going to go too far and Harris was going to kill him.

He struggled to his feet, surprised to see the trailers gone and the fairgrounds dark. Shouts from the Carnies drifted through the night air as they locked up and returned to their mobile homes. Where had Harper taken the girls?

Head pounding, he stumbled through the dark to his squad car. Lawson would give him hell if he didn't return it before going home, but he'd deal with him in the morning. Right now, he needed an aspirin and a stiff drink.

His pocket vibrated with the ringing of his cell phone. Tough. Anyone calling him right now would only yell, and his head couldn't stand the noise. He licked his lips, tasting blood, and cursed as he slid behind the steering wheel of his car. Yep. One of these days, he was going to be the big man on top and the others would do *his* bidding.

All he had to do until then was get rid of the blond thorn in his side and her DEA sidekick.

CHAPTER FIFTEEN

Loud banging on her door the next morning had Lacey reaching for her weapon. When had that become second nature to her?

"We're going to church," John called through the door.

Lacey groaned and relaxed back on the pillows, leaving her gun on the nightstand. A quick peek at the clock showed she'd barely gotten five hours of sleep. She bolted to a sitting position. Church?

"Wait! What?" She lurched toward the door and opened it. "You go to church?"

John stopped halfway down the hall, then turned. "I used to go all the time. Alice told me last night that the Harpers attend faithfully. So, that means we go too. We're leaving in an hour. Dress is casual." He flashed her a grin and continued on his way.

He had to stop doing that. They were in the middle of a struggle to survive and one little grin from him sent her heart somersaulting. She had mental problems.

Sighing, she closed the door and moved to the closet to search for something suitable to wear to church, casual or not. With the burning of her grandfather's house, all she had with her was what she had in the suitcase. Which wasn't much.

A pair of clean jeans and a black long-sleeved tee-shirt. She left the room and headed for the master bedroom. When no one answered at her knock, she stepped inside and made a bee-line for the closet. Yes. John's sister-in-law wore the same size of clothes.

Lacey flipped through the items hanging on the rack and withdrew a navy sweater dress that would go nice with her ankle boots. Hopefully, John wouldn't mind her borrowing the things. She slipped the dress from the hanger, turned, and gasped.

John stepped from the master on-suite, a towel riding extremely low on his hips. "Whoa!" He ducked back into the bathroom. "You should knock."

Face flaming, Lacey turned around. "I did." She bit her lip to keep from smiling. What a view to wake up to. "Do you mind if I borrow some of your sister-in-law's clothes?"

"Take them all if you want. I haven't gotten around to taking them to charity."

Still smiling, Lacey strolled from the room. She'd known John was well-built, but hadn't realized how muscular he was, until she'd seen him in almost nothing. Wrong for her to dwell on or not, she was glad for the brief glimpse that brightened her morning. She'd deal with her embarrassment when they saw each other over breakfast.

She showered and slipped into the dress, feeling pretty for the first time since fleeing her home. She smoothed the dress over her hips, then ran a brush through her hair. Silly or not, it was nice to look like a woman again.

The aroma of bacon alerted her to the passing time. She slipped her gun into her purse. Was it wrong to attend church with a weapon? Then, hurried to the kitchen.

John's eyes twinkled when he met her gaze. "Good morning."

"Morning." She ducked her head. Must his voice sound so husky?

"I'm staying home with Meagan," Alice said, glancing between them. "I'm not going to put her in the nursery until this is all behind us. I don't trust the Harpers not to use her against you."

"I agree." John plucked a slice of bacon from the plate in front of him and popped it into his mouth. "Lacey and I are only going to let the Harpers know we aren't running scared."

"You're trying to draw them out of the woodwork," Lacey stated.

He nodded. "I want to see their reactions after last night. They have to know I took the girl."

"I guess we should be safe enough in God's house." Hopefully. She'd resumed her nightly prayer time the night before while trying to sleep, and while she hadn't felt His overpowering presence, she didn't feel quite so alone.

"I don't want you leaving my side, church or not," he said. "It may be God's house, but the vipers slither freely." He pushed to his feet. "We leave in fifteen minutes."

Lacey ate quickly, then sped to the bathroom to

brush her teeth. Fifteen minutes on the dot, John called her to join him in the truck. She grabbed her purse, and a woman's finely designed trench coat from the hall closet, and dashed outside.

"You sure don't like to be late, do you?" she said, sliding into the front passenger seat.

"No."

He turned the ignition and steered them toward town, eventually pulling up in front of a lovely, old-fashioned church complete with white paint and a steeple that reached for the autumn sky.

Lacey found it hard to believe that evil would dare step foot in such a quaint place. She shoved open her door, then glanced at John. "Should I leave my gun in the truck?"

He laughed. "Yes. I don't think you'll have to shoot anyone at church."

Relief flooded through her. She retrieved the gun and stashed it in the truck's glove compartment. "I'm ready."

"You act as if you're going to the guillotine."

"I really don't know what to expect from one day to the next." She slid from the truck. While she'd suspected something would happen at the fair because of John's suspicions, she didn't put it past her uncle to approach her at church. After all, he'd assaulted her in the crowded fairgrounds. Her face still had the marks to prove it, although a dead woman's makeup had helped hide the evidence. With John at her side, she felt confident enough to stare into the eyes of a snake and walk away unscathed.

He slipped her hand through the crook of his arm. "Let's keep up the pretense of boyfriend and girlfriend.

I like it."

Her face flushed. "I'll be the envy of every girl in town."

His laugh rang across the churchyard, drawing attention from those yet to enter the building. "I doubt that, but thank you for the compliment."

Inside, they chose seats toward the back of the sanctuary. Lacey slid in first, glancing around as she did so. The small building was filling up fast. She spotted the Harper men in the front row. So like Ben to choose a seat of privilege. A place that let everyone see how falsely pious he was. Next to him was his brother, the mayor, wearing a suit that probably cost more than Lacey charged to photo shoot a wedding.

After twenty minutes of singing hymns fashioned to more contemporary beats, she enjoyed forty minutes of a fabulous teaching on relying on God to lead you. The message particularly pricked at her conscience, considering she was bent on revenge for Aunt Ruth's death, but it gave her meat to chew on. Not to mention, she'd probably spend a lot of time each night warring with what she knew was the right thing to do and what she wanted to do.

She cast a sideways glance at John, whose gaze was glued on Harris. The big man sported a split lip and a bruised jaw. Something that happened the night before, perhaps?

"Wait for me by the sanctuary doors," John said, leading her from their pew. "I want to ask Lawson a few more questions. Do. Not. Leave this building under any circumstances."

She nodded and obediently stood where he pointed, again squelching the fact he ordered her rather than asked. A flaw of his she would have to learn to deal with.

The congregation surged past her. At one point, someone grabbed her hand, thrust a slip of paper into her palm, and disappeared before she could see who did it. She opened her hand and unfolded the white square.

"I'm watching you."

~

"Lawson." John jogged to the officer's car. "A minute, please."

The man frowned, but didn't get in his car. "I don't like being seen talking to you. Can't you call me?"

"Did Cherie get away okay?"

He nodded. "Two people from the safe house picked her up last night. She agreed to testify once we take this to court." He glanced over John's shoulder. "Now, unless you want everyone to know I'm helping you, don't come up to me in public." He opened his door and slid inside.

Shaking his head and doing his best to look as if he'd been scolded by the sergeant, John stormed back to the building and past the Harper men standing in the foyer. Without looking their way, he retrieved a pale-faced, trembling, Lacey and hurried back out.

Once inside the truck, he faced her. "What happened?"

She showed him a slip of paper. "In church. They gave this to me in a safe place."

"They're getting nervous. It's time to make a call to my supervisor."

"He'll tell you to stay out of it."

"Maybe, but it's time to get more help." He put his hand over hers. "I know you want the personal satisfaction of bringing these people down, but this goes back for generations. Won't it be enough to see it end?"

"I don't know." Her voice faded.

"Is it worth your life? Or mine?"

She took a deep, shuddering breath. "No. You're right. Let's call for help."

He knew it took a lot of effort for her to relinquish control. He was struggling with the concept himself. But, it was more important to put an end to the Harper men's reign than to feel the personal satisfaction of being the one to bring them down single-handedly. Still, it was a tough pill to swallow.

The trip home was made in silence. Once they returned, he filled Alice in on what had happened, then headed to his office to make the phone call.

"It's about time you called." His supervisor, Stephen Mansfield's, growl vibrated over the phone. "I've left you messages."

"Which I've ignored." John leaned back in his office chair. "But, now I'm ready to let you know the mess I've gotten myself into." He spent the next fifteen minutes telling a quiet Mansfield what was transpiring in Oak Grove.

"This is really deep trouble, Canyon."

"Yes, sir."

"Let me see what I can find out on my end. I'll get back with you tomorrow. Keep your head down, and your lady friend out of sight. I don't like this at all."

"I was thinking of heading up the mountain tomorrow to hunt for the farm. The weatherman is predicting snow in a few days. We won't be able to do much of anything if that happens."

"Are you saying you want off your leave of absence to work this case? What about your niece? What about returning here?"

"I've hired help for my niece. I can't return home until this is settled. I know it's out of our jurisdiction, but I'm going to work the case with or without your approval."

Mansfield sighed. "I figured as much. I'll talk to you tomorrow."

John let the legs of his chair fall back to the floor with a thump. There was no turning back now. He'd committed himself to seeing this through. Once word got out that he involved the DEA, things were going to get really nasty.

He rubbed his hands roughly over his face. Something needed to be done to keep Meagan and Lacey safe. He could send Alice away with the child, but it would be a waste of breath to tell Lacey to go.

As if his thoughts had conjured her, she stood in the doorway of his office. "I just got a call on my cell phone. It's from the same person who gave me the warning message that sent me running from my home."

He straightened. "What did they say?"

"That they are a friend of my aunt's, and there is something more hidden at my grandfather's farm. Something that will shed light on the murder from long ago."

He stared at her. Who was this mystery friend of Aunt Ruth's, and why did he, or she, care what was happening? "Do you have any idea where something might be hidden? The house is gone, the basement, too, most likely. I didn't see any outbuildings, other than a barn and a tin shed."

"There has to be something we've missed. I'm going over there tomorrow."

"*We're* going tomorrow. We'll check the land. Something has to be there." He stood. "I'll make sure the four-wheeler has gas. I don't want to take the horses, and I definitely don't want to be caught on foot if we have visitors."

He fully intended to have wheels and weapons.

CHAPTER SIXTEEN

The next morning, Lacey climbed onto the four-wheeler behind John and wrapped her arms around his waist. It was colder on the mountain than it had been below in town, but even through his down coat his body heat radiated through her. She was infatuated with the man, no doubt about it. Closing her eyes, she rested her cheek on his broad back.

The odor of charred wood greeted her before she set eyes on what was once her grandfather's pride and joy. She lifted her head and slid from the four-wheeler. It seemed fitting somehow that the odor remained, instead of dissipating on the mountain's winter wind.

"I'll keep my eyes peeled while you sift through the rubbish," John said. "Then, we'll head into the woods."

She nodded and kicked at a scorched beam. There wasn't anything to be found. She knew that without looking. Even the door to the storm shelter had burned through. At least she had managed to save the small chest with the photos.

She peered into the cellar. A black abyss stared back. Someone had cast aside the pieces of the door, signifying they'd gone down the cement block steps in search of … something. Another waste of time if Lacey followed. She turned to John.

"I'm ready. There's nothing left." She blinked back the tears burning her eyes and resumed her seat behind him.

They followed a barely-there path that cut through the trees and stopped at a small bluff overlooking a fast running creek. Across the water was a ladder leading into the branches of a thick oak tree. A small house nestled between two branches as big around as Lacey's legs.

"That ladder doesn't look old enough to have been here more than a year," John said, cutting the engine. "When did your grandfather die?"

"About a year ago. I didn't know him well, but Aunt Ruth came here at least once a month to visit." She stood. "Do you think what we're looking for is in there?"

"I do. The problem will be getting across that creek. The water has to be like ice."

She clapped him on the shoulder and grinned. "Unless you can build a bridge, it looks like you're going to get wet."

"It's your land." He put his hands on his hips and scanned the area. "Maybe a log will work." He marched to their right and pulled a long board from the bushes. "Here we go. I knew whoever put that tree house up would have a way to cross."

Lacey's eyes widened. There was no way she was crossing on a wobbly two-by-four. It was so long, it sagged in the middle.

John found a section of the creek the board fit across, then stomped on it with a booted foot. "Seems secure."

"I'll wait here." She swallowed against the sudden dryness in her throat.

"Nope. We stay together." He grabbed her hand. "Don't be a sissy. I won't let you fall in the water."

Fine. But she wasn't going up the tree.

She stepped onto the board. John shook his legs. She shrieked. "Stop!"

He laughed and steadied them, then let go of her hand and raced across.

She froze and narrowed her eyes. When she got her hands on him …

He grinned and scurried up the ladder like a ten-year-old boy hiding from his sister. "Are you going to stand there all day? You don't want to be stranded if your uncle comes." He ducked into the treehouse.

Good point. She inched her way across, forcing herself to refrain from kissing the ground once she reached the pine needle-covered soil. She glanced up. "Find anything?"

"A metal cigar box that looks very promising." He poked his head out. "Catch." He dropped it.

Lacey sprang forward. The box fell into her hands, surprising her with its weight. She blew away the dust and lifted the lid. Inside lay several newspapers and a journal. Hope sprang in her chest. This had to be what they were looking for.

She met John's satisfied gaze. "Come on. Let's get this box home."

He jumped from the tree, landing on both feet, and

grabbed her around the waist. He spun her until she grew dizzy. "We're almost there, Lacey. Can you feel it?"

"I can." She smiled into his face. The presence of her Aunt Ruth seemed to settle around her shoulders like a beloved shawl. Justice was so close, Lacey could smell its sweet fragrance. "Now, put me down, you crazy fool."

His gaze settled on her lips. He loosened his grip, letting her slide down the length of him. The metal box was the only thing between them. She licked her lips, waiting for his kiss.

A twig snapped.

~

John shoved Lacey behind him, relaxing when a rabbit bounded across the path. "Let's go."

What was he thinking? He'd almost put them at risk. For what? A kiss? He could steal one of them from the safety of the house. He needed to keep focused. Romantic distractions could get them both killed.

He raced them back to the house. The hunt for the marijuana farm could wait until tomorrow. If they were lucky, the box clutched against Lacey's chest could hold all the answers they were looking for.

On the ride back, he tried not to think how good it felt with her arm around his waist. How soft she was plastered against his back. Or how badly he had wanted to kiss her and how good she had felt in his arms.

Lacey wasn't the typical type of woman he once found himself attracted to. She was the type a man settled down with. He couldn't fool around with her. The danger needed to pass, justice needed to be served, then he could explore a possible future with the woman sitting behind him.

He drove the four-wheeler into the garage and shut off the engine. "Let's go see what treasures we found."

Lacey slid from the back of the vehicle and marched toward the house, leaving John to secure the garage door. He didn't mind. He understood her excitement. In fact, anticipation boiled inside him like sparkling cider. The newspapers in the box had appeared old. Perhaps old enough to explain a murder from generations ago.

He loped to the house and joined the women at the kitchen table. Alice informed him that Meagan was down for a nap, and sandwiches were in the fridge. He grabbed two thick ham and cheese and sat.

"Let's see what's in the box," he told Lacey.

She pulled out two newspapers, yellowed with age, and a journal. The book's pages were held together with twine. She slid the newspapers to him and untied the string from the journal.

"It belongs to a Boomer Lawson." She raised her head and speared him with a glance. "Any relation to the sergeant?"

"That is a very good question." One John intended to ask at his first opportunity. If he was related, it helped the sergeant's remarks about having his own reasons for being in Oak Grove make more sense. The big man might be there for a bit of justice of his own.

He opened a newspaper dated June 10, 1929. On the front page was an article about the hanging of one black man. The next paper stated his name as Boomer Lawson, stating he left behind a wife and two young sons. The authorities had no suspects.

"Boomer states here that a police officer, Colvin

Harper, shot and killed a young man that stumbled across his still," Lacey said. "Then," she flipped a page, "the next day says that the blacks who live along the river bottom were planning to exact revenge. Boomer tried to talk them out of it. Two more men were killed. Shot down by Harper." She frowned. "It looks to me as if Harper wanted to clean out an entire community of people. Any way he could. There's also a few references to visits made by the KKK. No wonder the Harpers don't want this information to get out. We may still live in the south, but thankfully, times have changed. This type of conduct isn't allowed anymore."

"I agree. This would definitely keep Roy from being reelected." John refolded the papers. "The only thing left to do is find the farm." Then, they'd have enough information on the Harpers to prevent them from ever committing another crime. They'd be behind bars for a very long time.

"What do we do with the old information? Can we use it to bribe the Harpers into a confession? Ben and Roy weren't the ones who killed those black men."

"Unfortunately, this info is only good for dangling over the Harpers' heads as incentive to stay out of our way."

"Or cause them to be more determined to kill you," Alice added. "I'm going with that."

John agreed. They needed to keep quiet about the journal. He'd turn it all over to his supervisor and let him take it from there. "At least we know why they're so dead set on shutting Lacey up. I believe they think she had this information days ago."

"That, and the photos."

John's cell phone rang. He pulled it from his pocket

and glanced at the caller I.D. Mansfield. "I'll take this in the office." He stood and left the room, pressing the talk button. "What did you find out?"

"That you're in a big mess."

John closed his office door and sat at his desk, shutting out the sound of Lacey following him. She'd be madder than a wet cat at him closing her out, but he wanted to see where things stood with Mansfield first. "Like what?"

"The sergeant out there? He requested to be transferred from St. Louis to that po-dunk town. Seems he has roots there."

"We discovered that today. I haven't had the opportunity to speak with him yet." He filled Mansfield in on what else they'd found. "Tomorrow, we'll search for the farm. Once we find it, I'll call you for backup."

"Make sure you do. I don't want you going in guns blazing with no more support than a photographer."

~

Ben cursed and yanked the earpiece out of his ear. While Harris had made good on his promise to plant some recording devices in Canyon's farmhouse before arriving at the fairgrounds, Ben didn't like hearing that those in the house had the information they needed to sully the Harper name. Nor was he excited in the slightest about them bringing in the DEA.

His gut reaction was to make sure they met with a group of armed men when they discovered the farm. His brain told him it was better to have everyone cleared out. A showdown would only bring in the troops faster. The Harpers wouldn't have time to prepare. They needed to come up with a plan to retaliate and douse whatever flames Lacey's accusations would rise up once she brought everything out into the open.

If they could discount her credibility in some way … It was the twenty-first century, but Oak Grove was a small town run on old-fashioned values. Maybe he could play up the aspect of her living with Canyon. Put a few well-placed barbs among the women at church.

He threw his coffee mug across the room. It would never work. That old bag living there was enough of a chaperone to dispel any rumors. The only thing to do was kill them all.

But … it had to look like an accident.

CHAPTER SEVENTEEN

Lacey woke the next morning to the sound of music. Literally. Her ring tone on her cell phone was Julie Andrews's voice.

She fumbled for the phone. "Hello?"

"I need you to meet me at the Oak Grove library at nine a.m.," the mysterious voice said.

"Who is this?" She scooted to a sitting position. The caller was responsible for Lacey fleeing her home, and this was now the third time they'd contacted her.

"If you want justice for Ruth, you'll meet me." Click.

Lacey tossed aside the thick comforter and raced barefooted to John's room. "Get up!" She pounded on the door.

"What?" A tousle-haired, sleepy-eyed John wearing faded plaid pajama bottoms opened the door.

Tearing her gaze away from his chiseled chest, she held up her phone. "The caller wants to meet me at the library at nine."

John squinted. "That's in four hours. Wake me in two." He closed the door.

Her mouth opened and closed a few times before she realized he was serious about going back to sleep. Cold from the floor seeped into her feet. While she knew she wouldn't be able to sleep, she headed back to her room anyway, passing a blinking-eyed Alice.

"Sorry to wake you." Lacey gave her an apologetic grin, then closed her door.

How could John not be on pins and needles? She sat on the edge of the bed, knowing it was a waste of time to try getting even an hour of sleep.

She reached for the wooden chest and dumped out the photos. She ran her forefinger over her aunt's face. "We're close, Ruth. So close to stopping Ben."

After the death of Lacey's parents, people who had loved her, but believed in self-sufficiency for their child and were gone a lot, Ruth had been Lacey's anchor. She hadn't deserved the death she'd gotten.

Lying back on the mattress, Lacey stared at the ceiling. Her heart ached with missing the woman who had taught her what it meant to be a responsible adult. A woman who cared for people. A Godly woman that followed God. None of which Lacey had done lately. Her aunt would be disappointed if she were here.

Still, Lacey struggled with a loving God that would take away the only person in the world Lacey had left. And, in such a violent way. But, Ruth would have said His ways were not theirs and sometimes man wasn't meant to know the answers that side of heaven.

She wiped her eyes. She might as well fix breakfast for everyone. She pushed to her feet and made her way to the kitchen. Omelets were her specialty and it had been a long time since she'd cooked for anyone other than herself.

It wasn't long before the house filled with the aroma of frying bacon and the others filed into the room. John had Meagan on his hip and looked way too sexy for that early in the morning. He was going to make a wonderful father for the little girl, and a great husband for some lucky woman.

"Sorry I brushed you off earlier," he said, buckling Meagan into her highchair. "I don't do well when I'm woken abruptly."

"No problem. I'm assuming you're going with me?" She slid an omelet onto a plate and handed it to him.

"Not directly. I'll be there, but out of sight. We don't want to scare this person away." He handed the plate to Alice and held out his hand for another.

Once they all had their omelets, Meagan with scrambled eggs and bite-sized pieces of toast, they sat around the table. She'd been hungry when she'd started cooking, but now that the food was in front of her, all Lacey could think about was the upcoming meeting.

By the time she was dressed and in the truck, her nerves twanged like a fiddle. When they reached town, she perspired under her sweatshirt. She chewed on her cuticle until John pulled her hand from her mouth.

"I'm going to have to drop you off around the corner," he said. "We can't risk the caller seeing me." He handed her a small silver disc. "Put this behind your ear and keep your hair down. I'll be able to hear everything that goes on. If you run into trouble, I'll be right there."

"Where did you get this?" The man was full of surprises.

"I have a few tricks." He planted a quick kiss on her cheek. "Good luck."

She nodded and exited the truck. As she made her way to the library, she had no idea who she was looking for. A woman, most likely. But, the building would be full of women. She opened the double glass doors and stepped inside.

The pleasant smell of books and air conditioning, even on a chilly autumn day, greeted her. A middle-aged woman smiled from behind the counter. Two other women browsed the table with a sign that stated "New Releases". None of these were who Lacey looked for.

She headed for the back of the large room and strolled up and down the nonfiction titles, hoping someone would call her by name. No one did. After twenty minutes, she sat at an empty table and fought the urge to talk to John through the earpiece. She didn't want to attract attention by seeming to talk to herself. After another ten minutes, she sighed and went to the women's restroom. If she didn't locate the caller soon, she'd consider the morning a total waste of time.

"Lacey Baxter?"

She whirled.

The woman from the counter held out an envelope. "Someone left this for you."

"Thank you." She grabbed the envelope and rushed to the restroom.

Inside, she made a beeline for the handicap stall. She thrust the door open, barged inside, and screamed. Sitting on the toilet, fully clothed and covered in blood, was a woman around her aunt's age. The woman's throat had been cut.

Changing direction, Lacey sped back out of the restroom. "I'm coming," she told John. "The caller is dead. I repeat, the caller is dead." She slammed through the doors and into the parking lot.

~

John was speeding toward the library before he spotted Lacey fleeing across the lot. He screeched to a halt. "Get in."

She yanked open the door and jumped in.

They were moving before her door was closed. "What happened?" he asked.

"The librarian gave me an envelope. I had almost given up." She took a deep shuddering breath. "Then, I went to the restroom to have some privacy while I read it. That's where I found the body."

"So, you haven't opened it?"

She shook her head. She opened her mouth to speak and shrieked instead as a bullet shattered the back windshield. Folding her arms over her head, she ducked.

John whipped the steering wheel to the right, taking them down a narrow road. "We're going to Lawson."

"Is it safe?"

"Safer than going home. At least until we shake whoever is shooting at us." Actually, neither location seemed ideal, but the police department was preferable over being on the road.

They stopped in front of the police station. John ran around to the passenger side as a black SUV, horns blaring, raced past. Two final shots rang out before John ducked behind the truck.

It had only been a warning. If their pursuer had wanted them dead, they would have been.

Before they entered the station, Lawson, gun in hand, ran out. "What in the …?"

"Someone shot at us. And, there's a dead body in the women's restroom of the library."

"Come again?"

John repeated himself. "Want us to follow you to the library?"

"No, you'll ride with me." He led them toward a navy-colored Suburban. As he drove, he radioed the station and told them to send another car.

"It'll be Harris, but he's all we've got," Lawson said. "The idiot will pretend he doesn't know anything and the charade will continue."

"We know that Boomer was your grandfather," Lacey said, turning the envelope over in her hands. "That's why you're here, right? For the same reason John and I are?"

He held the vehicle door open for her, then glanced at John. "We'll talk later. While I drive, you can tell me why you were at the library. Somehow, I don't think you were there to check out books."

John climbed into the front passenger seat, leaving the back for Lacey. He explained about the phone calls she'd been getting and about the requested meeting.

"What's in the envelope?" Lawson glanced in his rearview mirror.

"I haven't opened it." She handed it over the seat to John. "I can't. A woman died because of this."

John took it from Lacey and ripped open the envelope, despite Lawson's protests about fingerprints. Lacey's were already all over it. His wouldn't matter at this point. He pulled out a single sheet of paper and read:

Dear Lacey:

I'm sorry to be so mysterious, but Ruth asked that if anything suspicious should happen to her that I would tell you to run as far from Ben Harper as possible. You didn't run far enough.

The Harpers will stop at nothing to protect their name and their enterprise. They have their hands in so many illegal dealings they make Capone look like a Boy Scout.

There is a safety deposit box, number 137, at the bank in your name. You should have found the gold key at your grandfather's house. Taped evidence, retrieved from Ruth during one of your uncle's business dinners, is inside the box. That should be all of the evidence you need.

If you're reading this letter, they are getting too close to me for comfort. Pray they don't get to you.

Sue Ellingham

"I have that key. I wondered what it went to. But, I do have a question. How did anyone know we were going to the library?" Lacey asked.

Lawson glanced at John. "Have you checked your house for bugs?"

John pounded the dashboard. Idiot. They would have had time while he and the others were at the fair.

~

That was the most fun Harris had had in a long time. It would have been easy for the first bullet to have gone into Lacey's head, but that wasn't exactly the accident the Harpers wanted to have happen.

He tilted the bottle of whiskey he clutched and took a long drag. Who cared if he was on duty? So what if he wasn't exactly following orders by shooting up the highway? A man needed a little rest and relaxation. Crime was hard work. Especially when the men you worked for wanted you to do all their dirty dealings while they stayed in their nice houses with their beautiful women and all their money keeping their hands clean.

Life wasn't fair. There were those who did the work and those who gave the orders. He took another swig of his drink, swerving a bit on the blacktop. But sometimes, those lower on the ladder managed to climb their way to the top. That would be him. It was just a matter of time.

A few weeks at the most. Then, the town would see who the top dog really was.

The temperature was dropping quickly. It actually looked like snow, and it was only October. How awful if a winter storm moved in and somehow the Canyon farm lost all their power and heat. Wouldn't that be sad if they were all to freeze to death?

He laughed and tossed the empty bottle out the window. Yep, Larry Harris was about to become a big man on campus. He increased his speed and headed for home. He needed to wash the blood off his hands.

CHAPTER EIGHTEEN

Lacey waited in the library's atrium while John and Lawson viewed the body. One look was enough for her. Several onlookers craned their necks as the library security guard ushered them outside, then took up his stance in front of Lacey. Even a balding sixty-something-year-old with pepper spray was better protection than none.

"So, you found her?"

Lacey nodded. Maybe she was wrong about it being better to have someone with her, if that someone was going to insist on a conversation.

"Just sitting on the toilet?"

"Yep." She strained to peer around him. *Come on, John.*

"Must have been a shock."

"You have no idea."

He proceeded to regale her with tales of his military days and the time he found a rotting cow in the desert of Afghanistan. She sighed and leaned against the desk placed there for donated books. How did a dead cow relate to a dead woman? Especially a woman trying to help Lacey get justice for Aunt Ruth's death?

To occupy her mind while the guard droned on, she focused on the fact there might be recording devices planted in John's home. Thank goodness, they'd been in the squad car when John read the letter from Sue Ellingham. At least the Harpers wouldn't know about the safety deposit box.

Her heart leaped to think they were close to putting an end to the evil that creeped through Oak Grove. Soon, the Harpers could no longer lord it over the town's citizens, doing whatever their evil hearts desired in order to line their pockets.

The restroom door opened and Sue's body, zipped into a body bag, was rolled out on a gurney. Lacey was ripped from her thoughts at seeing how a woman had so violently died for trying to help her.

"A real pity, that," the guard said. "A shame when someone is killed. Must have been a transient. Sometimes, they slip into the library between the time I give the final check and when I lock the doors."

It wasn't a transient, but Lacey held her tongue. Let him believe what he would. She stepped forward and followed John outside.

He gave her a sad smile. "Lawson is going to take us to get the Jeep, then follow us home so we can search for bugs. Are you alright?"

"Sad for Sue." She exhaled sharply. "But curious as to what might be in the deposit box."

"We'll go there after we clean house. I know it's closer than home, but I don't want any more said without checking that we aren't being spied on."

"I understand. The key is in my room, anyway." Still, she really wanted to know what was in the box.

After Sue's body was loaded into a waiting ambulance, Lacey, John, and Lawson returned to the police station and retrieved her Jeep. The drive back home was silent, she and John lost in their own thoughts.

John drove with one hand draped loosely over the steering wheel, the other stroking his chin. She wanted to ask what he was thinking, but didn't want to disturb his thoughts if he were trying to make sense of all the evidence being tossed at them. There would be time for talking later. She sighed and stared out the window.

At home, she stepped aside and let John and Lawson enter the house ahead of her. John held a finger to his lips, signaling that there be no talking, and the men began their search.

Alice's eyes widened for a moment, then she nodded in understanding. "I think I'll put a pot roast in the oven for dinner. Lacey, could you help me in the kitchen?"

"Sure," she said, a little too loudly, which elicited a grin from John. He must think her an idiot.

"I'm dying to hear about your new recipe," Alice said, banging pans she fished from the cupboard. "Maybe you could write it down for me?"

Lacey grabbed a pad of paper from next to the phone and told Alice about finding Sue Ellingham dead.

Alice closed her eyes and sighed deeply, then wrote, "I knew Sue. A wonderful woman." She ripped the paper from the pad and turned on the stove, lighting the sheet on fire from the burner. "That recipe has been around for a long time. Used by a lot of people." She swiped the back of her hand across her eyes.

One more good person whose death needed justice. Lacey shook her head. When would it end? She sat at the table and buried her head in her hands. Everything in her wanted to confront Ben. To storm to his house, her aunt's house, and demand he confess to killing her.

She lifted her head when Alice plunked a mug of coffee in front of her. She patted Lacey's head as if she were Meagan's age, then measured grounds for another pot.

"I'm sure John will want fresh coffee when he's finished in the … barn."

Lacey forced a smile. "Thank you. Who is taking care of your place? You're here every day, twenty-four hours a day taking care of Meagan."

"I hired someone to take care of what little I kept. When my husband died, I sold off most of the livestock. Not much left other than some chickens, and a couple of goats. I spend most of my time puttering in the flower beds during the spring and working on crafts for the annual church fundraiser. I stay busy, but this is an exciting change of pace." She sat across from Lacey. Placing her hand over Lacey's, she mouthed, "It will be all right."

~

John moved framed pictures from the fireplace mantel. Nothing. He glanced inside lamp shades, under doilies, and in candy dishes. Still nothing. Why had his sister-in-law insisted on so many knick-knacks? Did a country home have to be cluttered to be homey? All the stuff did was make it harder to find something hidden.

"This is going to take all afternoon," he said.

Lawson held a finger to his lips, then knelt and peered under the sofa. He huffed and shook his head. Standing in the center of the room, he planted beefy fists on his hips and turned in a slow circle. He grinned and pantomimed for a screwdriver.

John rushed to the kitchen and rummaged in a drawer, withdrawing a screwdriver with interchangeable heads. He shook his head at the questions in the women's eyes and hurried back to Lawson.

Seconds later, Lawson had removed the electrical outlet cover next to the living room arch and held a small recording device in his hand. An hour later, after removing every outlet cover in the house, they found five more. There had been one in every bedroom and in the living room and dining room. John couldn't wait to squeeze his hands around Harper's neck.

He dropped the devices into a small cardboard box. Lawson carried them out to the trunk of his squad car and returned to the house for sandwiches and coffee.

"You found six?" Lacey glanced up as John entered the kitchen. "No wonder they've been one step ahead of us this whole time."

"Are you sure they're gone?" Alice asked.

"Yes." Lawson entered the room and sat at the table. "And," he winked, "since we're clear, I suggest you set up a meeting with your informant for tomorrow."

"The park? Two o'clock?" John could play along.

"Sounds good. I'm sure you can handle things without me. Now, I'm starving." He patted his hard stomach. "You promised to feed me."

"So I did." Alice set a plate with two thick ham and

cheese sandwiches in front of him. "There's more if you want it."

"Now that you're filling your belly," John accepted his own plate of food, "how about you tell us more about your grandfather. I've found out that you requested to be transferred here."

"You sure know how to ruin a man's appetite." He took a huge bite of his sandwich. "Grandpap was against alcohol in any form. Grandma said he swore it made a man's brain turn to mush. Then, when he speaks out about it because of an innocent man's death, he's hung. I've been digging into the past a bit, and come across some information that sent me here. Grandpap wasn't who we thought he was." He grinned, his teeth white against his dark skin. "Seems I'm after the same group of men you two are."

"Then why act so surprised when Lacey and I approached you the first time?"

"I don't want you blowing my cover." He finished off one sandwich and started on another. "If I can keep the Harpers convinced I'm willing to look the other way, it helps me."

"We all know Harris is as dirty as a white dog in the mud."

"Yes, we do. I've got a file at my house two inches thick on the man." Lawson wiped his mouth with a napkin. "Don't worry. We're almost ready to drop the hammer."

"Unfortunately, more people may die." Like Lacey.

"My suggestion is that you get to the safety deposit box, let me know what it contains, and then hole up here until things come to a boil." He pushed away from the table. "This isn't your jurisdiction. You're

California DEA. This will stand up better in court if I bring them down. You're helping off the record. Thanks for the lunch." He marched from the house and out to his car.

"I really hope you're right about trusting him," Lacey said, collecting the plates. "Our lives are in his big hands."

"We can trust him." John recognized a good man when he saw one. "Since he wants justice as much as we do, he'll do everything in his power to make sure it happens."

"I hope so. I agreed to follow your lead. I can only pray I don't regret it." She set the plates in the sink and left the room.

"It's hard for her to let go," Alice said. "She'll do fine."

"I hope so. We need to all be on the same page. If she decides to do something on her own …" He hated to think of the consequences. He was quickly falling for the beautiful blond. A world without her in it wasn't very appealing.

~

"They found the listening devices," Harris told Ben over the phone.

"You know this how?"

"I don't hear anything." Harris sat in an unmarked police car down the road from Canyon's house. "Normally, I can hear a pin drop."

"That's because you went and killed that woman!" He cursed. "Doing that alerted them to the fact that you had to be listening. Otherwise, you wouldn't have known. Stop acting on your own!" Click.

Harris punched the dashboard. Harper treated him

like a child. Killing the old woman was a message to the blond. Give him some credit. He had a brain and knew how to use it. He didn't need micro-managed.

~

Ben slammed the phone receiver down. Imbecile. He needed to be disposed of. Immediately. The man was going to ruin everything. He dialed Roy.

"We've got to get rid of Harris."

"Suggestion?"

"A shootout between him and Canyon? Then, my bullet will look like part of the fight."

"Sounds reasonable. When do you propose doing this? You could always cut his brake lines."

"That's too conspicuous. Harris already did it twice." He twirled in his office chair. "Weatherman is predicting snow later this week. That most likely means that Canyon will be snowed in. I'll tell Harris to formulate his plan of attack. Then, I'll dispose of him."

"As long as you realize that getting rid of him means you have to dirty your hands."

His hands were already dirty. He'd sullied them pushing Ruth over the cliff. "No problem."

"Make sure and get rid of the Canyon household at the same time. This fiasco has gone on long enough." Click.

Getting rid of them would be harder, but Ben was convinced he could do it. A few calls to St. Louis could have an army camped on Canyon's doorstep. Then, he'd get rid of Harris and the others from the comfort of his warm home.

Roy was wrong. Ben wouldn't have to touch the trigger. Money always found someone willing to do the dirty work.

CHAPTER NINETEEN

Lacey clutched the safety deposit key so tightly in her fist that it cut into her hand. What were they going to find that would put an end to all this?

"Ready?" John stopped the truck in front of the bank.

She nodded and slipped the key into the pocket on her chambray shirt. She slid from the truck before John could open the door for her and squared her shoulders. Taking a deep breath, she marched toward the double glass doors of the bank.

"Anxious?" John jogged to her side and opened the bank's front door.

"Very." She glanced up at him. "This could end it all."

"It could." He smiled. "I hope so."

In a different time, a different place, a girl could get lost in eyes the color of a spring sky. But now was not that time. She wrenched her gaze away and entered the bank.

"I'd like to open box 137," she said, approaching a man behind the customer service counter.

"Do you have your key?" he asked.

Lacey withdrew it from her pocket.

"Follow me."

He led them through a polished oak door and into a room lined with metal boxes in the wall. He pulled out one marked 137, inserted a key, then stepped back for Lacey to do the same. Once the box was open, he said, "I'll leave you alone. Let me know when you're ready to lock it up." He left the room.

Lacey took a deep breath and lifted the lid. Inside was a padded envelope. She pulled out the envelope and turned it upside down in her hand. A jump drive fell out. Her heart beat faster. Whatever was on the drive would put the Harpers behind bars.

"We have it," she whispered.

"Let's go." John took her by the elbow. "I don't trust anyone at this point, and the bank employee could be calling Roy Harper right this minute."

She dropped the drive and the key into her pocket. "Thank you," she called, as John ushered her outside and into the truck.

Once in, he gunned the engine and peeled from the parking lot.

"Do you really think the employee is in cahoots with Harper?"

"Yes. The look on his face when you asked for box 137 was not that of a non-interested person. My guess is … someone is on their way to the bank right now."

"But, no one knew about the box." She glanced over her shoulder to see whether they were being followed.

"But they know about us."

Not even the low temperature outside chilled her as much as his words.

He reached over and gripped her hand. "Don't worry. I'll take care of you."

She gave a shaky smile. "Who will take care of you?"

"Hopefully, Lawson." He parked in front of the police station, a place that was quickly becoming home away from home.

Lacey exited the truck. The jump drive seemed to burn through the fabric of her shirt and into her skin. John grasped her hand. They walked side-by-side into the building.

"He hasn't come in this morning," the receptionist said when they asked for the sergeant. "Neither has Harris. We'll be in a real fix if something happens."

"This is unusual for him?" John asked.

She nodded. "It's normal for Sergeant Lawson to call if he's going to be late. Harris? He's lazy. We're lucky if he doesn't show up."

This couldn't be good. Lacey's heart dropped to her knees. What if John was wrong about Lawson? What if he were, right now, on his way to the house to stop them from listening to the drive?

Her vision narrowed and she clutched John's arm. "Let's go. You can try to call him."

A sense of urgency tugged at the center of her. Trouble was coming. They didn't want to be caught out in the open.

John scribbled his phone number on a slip of paper and handed it to the receptionist. "If you hear from him."

Lacey pulled him along after her. "I want to go. Now. Something doesn't feel right."

"Okay."

They hurried back to the truck and sped for home. Lacey kept an eye on the road behind them the entire way, expecting another vehicle to roar up behind them, shooting through the window.

Her anxiety didn't lessen when they arrived at the house without incident. The trouble was coming. Whether that day or the next, she didn't know. But, it was coming.

~

The moment they stepped into the house, John held out his hand for the jump drive. "We'll listen to it on my laptop."

Lacey dropped it into his hand.

"What's happening?" Alice, Meagan on her hip, stepped from the kitchen.

"Lawson and Harris are both MIA," John said.

"You think Harris killed him?"

He shook his head. "I hope not. I hope Lawson is tagging him and that's why he didn't show for work. I'll meet you in the kitchen."

He retrieved his laptop from his office and set it on the kitchen table. He inserted the jump drive, clicked on the file, and sat back to listen.

"I'm telling you, she has photos."

"That's Ben," Lacey said.

"What's a few pictures?"

"That's Roy," Alice added. "Someone taped a conversation between them."

"Ruth?" Lacey glanced up.

"Hush." They couldn't hear if they were talking.

John turned up the volume on the laptop.

"They're of me in … compromising positions," Ben said. "She hinted around the other day that she knew what we were up to and was going to the authorities. What do you want me to do?"

"Kill her. But make it look like an accident."

Lacey gasped and clapped a hand over her mouth.

Silence filled the room for a few minutes, then Ben spoke again. "She's been spending a lot of time up in the attic. I found some old newspapers. She's digging around about what happened in 1929."

Roy cursed. "Finish her fast. See if the niece knows anything. If you even suspect that she does, kill her, too."

The recording ended, leaving the listeners in stunned silence.

"I knew he killed her," Lacey said, collapsing into a chair, "but to hear it—"

"This is all the evidence we need to convict them." John turned off his computer and ejected the jump drive. "I had planned on finding the farm tomorrow, but that might not be necessary."

"I think it might." Alice sat Meagan in her seat. "I saw a squad car go zooming past earlier today. Now, you say Lawson is missing. What if he's gone up there and needs your help?"

"Good point. We're leaving in fifteen minutes. Lacey, we're taking the horses. It'll be easier to sneak up on anyone guarding the place."

She nodded and hurried down the hall to her room.

"I wish you had someone more experienced with you," Alice said. "Maybe Lacey should stay and watch the child."

John put his hands on her shoulders. "I need *you* to protect her. She's more important than I am." It wasn't that he didn't believe in Lacey, he did. His heart told him she would come through in a pinch. But, to be safe, he wanted an experienced person with a gun watching over his niece.

"It's supposed to snow by dark. If you aren't home by then, you'll be caught out in it." Alice stepped back. "They're saying it's a bad storm come early."

"We'll be back by supper, whether we find the farm or not. Will you pack us a lunch?"

She nodded and turned to the fridge.

John hurried to his room, checking that he had extra ammunition and warm clothes for when the temperature dropped further. Was Lawson up the mountain? Was he alive? Was the farm vacant? So many questions. At least some had been answered with the jump drive. Lacey now knew without a doubt who killed her aunt. While he was pretty certain the Harpers were also behind the death of his brother and sister-in-law, he didn't have the certainty she did.

He shoved what he needed in a backpack and headed for the kitchen. Lacey was there, adding water and sandwiches to a pack of her own.

"Ready?" He asked.

"Yes." She patted the pocket of her coat. "Gun, ammo, camera, and backpack."

Less than half an hour later, they were riding the horses into the forest and up the mountain. If Lawson had taken the road, John had a good idea where he might have parked the car. The road ended on the other side of the mountain near the top. The big man would have had to walk from there. It at least gave John and

Lacey a starting point for their search.

"I don't think I'm equipped for a gunfight," Lacey said from behind him. "I've only fired a gun a few times in my life."

"I hope it doesn't come to a fight." The idea of her fighting anyone scared the dickens out of him. He should have come alone, but two pairs of eyes sometimes made all the difference. He glanced over his shoulder. Plus, he enjoyed having her with him. He only prayed that decision wouldn't result in his losing her.

They found the squad car exactly where he thought they would. He motioned for Lacey to dismount and be quiet, then made his way to the car. It was empty, the driver's door left open. Not that he had expected to see Lawson inside. He turned and scanned the ground for prints, hunching into his coat for warmth. It had gotten cold very quickly.

A set of footprints led to the right. Gun drawn, he followed, keeping Lacey behind him. They hadn't gone far before a gunshot rang out. He grabbed Lacey and threw her to the ground, covering her body with his.

~

Harris stared down at his boss. "Should I finish him off?"

"No." Ben yanked gloves over his hands. "The cold will soon enough. I heard something in the woods. It's either an animal or his backup. Let's get out of here."

"I need a cover story for the station." Harris hitched his pants. "Someone is going to wonder why neither Lawson or I came into work."

"You don't owe anyone an explanation." Idiot. "Keep your mouth shut, act ignorant, which shouldn't be difficult for you, and proceed as normal."

"One of these days you're going to regret talking to me that way."

Ben whirled, putting his face inches from Harris. He poked the fat man in the chest, his finger sinking into pudgy flesh as if in a loaf of bread. Disgusting. "Are you threatening me? Because, the mayor and I have a way of getting rid of threats. Don't forget where your meal ticket comes from."

Harris slapped his hand away. "I don't make idle threats. I make promises."

Ben pulled his revolver from its holster and pointed it at Harris's head. "One more word and I'll pull this trigger."

Harris pulled his weapon and trained it on Ben. "I guess we're checkmate."

A twig snapped.

Ben scowled. "Put that away. We have to go. We'll finish this conversation another time."

He raced for the four-wheelers. If there *was* a next time. The fat man puffing behind him had made his last independent thought. A thought that signed his death warrant as far as Ben was concerned. Him and Roy needed to erase their trail and find a new place to settle. Oak Grove, even after they eliminated Lacey Baxter and John Canyon, had gotten too hot.

He turned the ignition to the four-wheeler and roared away, leaving Harris to come or get caught. It didn't matter one way or the other to him. Hopefully, no one would find the sergeant until it was too late, if it wasn't already. If Canyon and Baxter were the ones in the woods, by the time they got the big man down the mountain and discovered what was waiting for them, they wouldn't be able to do much of anything, but wait to die.

CHAPTER TWENTY

Lacey struggled to free herself from John. "Are you shot?"

"No," he said, getting off her. "Are you?"

"No." Her cheek was scraped from where he threw her to the ground, but other than that, she was fine. Scared out of her mind, but physically okay.

John helped her to her feet before heading toward where the gunshot had come from. Did they really want to go there? Lacey brushed off her pants and followed, her heart in her throat and her gun clutched tight in her hand.

"What is it?" She tried to peer around John's broad shoulders. "Is anyone there?"

"Lawson's been shot." He stepped into a clearing and knelt next to the big man, placing his fingers along the man's neck. The officer's head bled, soaking the collar of his uniform. "He's still alive."

Lacey glanced around them, straining to hear any danger over the pounding of her heart. "We have to get out of here. They might come back."

"Agreed." John handed her his weapon. "I'll drag him into the shelter of the trees, then I'll need your help getting him to the four-wheeler."

There was no way all three of them were going to fit on the machine. She wouldn't let John stay behind. She'd rather run alongside than leave him to the fate of madmen with guns.

She stayed behind John and Lawson and backed into the trees, keeping her eyes peeled on the flattened dead grass across the clearing. She wasn't quite sure what she'd do if the vehicles that made the tracks reappeared, but she'd do her best to help John keep Lawson alive.

"I need you," John said. He held out his hand, wiggling his fingers for her to return his gun. "I'll heft him up, then we'll prop him under our arms. It will be slow going, but the temperature is dropping fast. If we leave him, he'll die."

Even with John helping, it took all of Lacey's strength to help lift Lawson. By the time they reached the four-wheeler, she dripped with perspiration despite the dropping temperatures. "It's starting to snow."

"We have to go." John glanced at the sky. "We'll be snowed in for a few days, according to the weatherman."

"But Lawson needs medical aid."

"It's a graze. Alice can patch him up." He propped Lawson on the vehicle, then climbed behind him. "I need you to perch on the rack, and hold on tight."

She swallowed against a throat gone dry and climbed on the thin metal rack. She'd no sooner shoved her gun into her pack and grabbed a hold with both hands, then John took them roaring down the mountain. Every bump they went over bit into her backside. Her fingers cramped from her tight grip.

"You okay back there?"

"No." A deep rut in the ground almost caused her to lose her seat. She bit her lip, drawing blood.

"I'm sorry, but Lawson needs help."

"I understand. Keep going." Her face grew numb from the cold and she blinked against the increasing fury of the storm. It wouldn't take much to make visibility almost zero. *Please, God, get us home safe.* Squinting, she peered up. Did He hear her anymore? She thought she'd felt His presence at church the other day and could only hope He smiled upon her as He once had. They would all need Him over the next few days.

After what seemed like an eternity, they pulled up to the back door of the house. Lacey helped John get Lawson inside.

"Call an ambulance," he told Alice.

"I guess you didn't go around by the road." She motioned her head toward the window. "We've got company and the phone lines are dead. I can't get a signal on any of the cell phones, either."

How was he supposed to call for backup? John sat Lawson in a chair, then moved to the front window. Lacey stayed close to his side.

Two black suburbans blocked the road. Four men on recreational vehicles made their way to the back of the house. They were surrounded.

"Idiots." John let the curtains fall into place. "Make sure all the doors and windows are locked. Put anything in front of the windows that can be moved, then tend to

Lawson. I'll head to my office and gather all the ammo."

Fear, as stark and cold as the snow falling outside the house, filled Lacey. She turned the lock on the back door, ignoring the man wearing a ski mask who peered in at her. She closed the sheers hanging over the small window. They were trapped. The men outside sat in wait until John and Lacey returned. What would they do if the men set fire to the house?

John returned and set two rifles and several boxes of ammo on the table. "Alice, if they start shooting, I need you to take Meagan to the secret room."

She shook her head. "You need me to fight. I'll put Meagan there, so she isn't hit by a stray bullet, but I'll return to help you."

It had come to this. Lacey sagged into a chair and stared at Lawson. His eyelids flickered. "He's waking up."

Alice filled a bowl with water and grabbed a rag from a drawer. "If that bullet had been a hair to the right, he wouldn't be sitting here. Did you find the farm?"

"No. We stopped looking when we found him." Lacey unzipped Lawson's heavy coat and pulled it off him. "Won't he need stitches?"

"Yep." Alice wiped away the blood, then peered closer at the spot the bullet had traveled. "He won't be the first man I've stitched up. There's a bottle of whiskey in the pantry that I brought up from the cellar. Fetch it, please. Then head to my room and get me my sewing kit."

Lacey nodded and hurried to do her bidding. Stitching someone up in the kitchen? Disinfecting with moonshine? What era were they living in?

~

Why were there men surrounding the house? Wouldn't it have been easier to kill John and Lacey when they were in the woods? What kind of game were the Harpers playing?

John loaded both rifles, then shoved the kitchen hutch in front of the front windows. It provided just enough room for the barrel of a rifle to stick through. He paused in his preparations and glanced to where the women doctored Lawson.

The view outside looked every bit like a gang war. John had a cellar full of moonshine. There was a marijuana farm within an hour or two's ride up the mountain. They were sitting on a powder keg of the mayor's making. To an outsider, it would look exactly like what he was seeing. He peered outside. Yep. The men looked like a swat team. They were being set up to die at the hands of hired men pretending to be law enforcement. No one would look twice to see that it was all a façade.

Lawson cursed and bolted to his feet, Alice's needle and thread hanging from his skin. "Are you trying to kill me?"

"I'm trying to save you, you big galoot. Now, sit!" She pointed at the chair. "You've lost a lot of blood and won't be any good to us if you pass out again."

"Why aren't I at the hospital?"

"Because, we're in the middle of a winter storm, we don't have cell reception, and the house is surrounded by men intent on killing us," John said. "Glad to see you're still among the living. What do you remember?"

"Stepping into a clearing. A shot rang out. That's

it." He hissed as Alice pulled the thread. "You're a sadist, woman."

"Hush. The more you fight me, the longer it will take."

"What do you mean we're surrounded?" he asked.

John explained the view outside the window. "I wonder when they'll make their move."

"Not until the snow stops. You should be able to get reception then," Lawson said, slapping Alice's hand away. "Enough. We're done. Tie a knot in it and step back."

"Fine." She did as instructed, gathered up her supplies, and left the room.

"Even if they try burning you out," Lawson said, "they'll have a tough time of it in this snowfall." He peered out the curtains, jumping back when a man's face appeared. "Brazen."

"There's some plywood in the cellar." John headed to the pantry and the open door in the back of it. "If you can, I could use some help boarding up the windows."

"It's better than sitting around while the women torture me." Lawson followed him down the steps and whistled at the sight of the whiskey still. "No wonder my grandpap was killed. No one likes their territory stepped on. And this is a lot of illegal brew." He ran his hands over the dirt walls. "Ole Boomer might have stood on the side of justice where murder was concerned, but he wasn't above making some money on the side."

John dragged a piece of plywood from behind the still. "I'll send Meagan and Lacey down here if shooting starts, or the house catches fire."

"Heck." Lawson chuckled. "I'll be hiding here, too.

Unless you know this room is here, you won't find it. They can burn the house to the ground and we'll walk out free when they leave."

"I don't know if I can do that." John dragged out another sheet of wood. "I want these men behind bars. We have a taped conversation between Ben and Roy discussing murdering Ruth. That's enough, even without the farm. This has to end. Now." They only had to live long enough to get the jump drive to the proper authorities. Once he'd made the house as safe as he could for the time being, he'd try calling his supervisor and request backup.

"You need to think of the women and that child." Lawson crossed his massive arms. "If the house is set on fire, we all come down here. Then, we come out and hunt down the men responsible. We can't do that if we're dead."

John leaned against the wall. He was right. John was thinking like Lacey, bent on revenge over justice. Did it matter how the men were prosecuted, as long as they were?

"You're right. Let's get the windows covered and wait to see what happens." God help them all.

~

Ben stomped the snow from his feet and climbed into the waiting SUV. Let the men he'd hired stay and freeze. He rolled the window down an inch. "Don't let them leave this house alive," he told Harris. "I'm heading home. I'll be back in the morning."

"You want us to stay here through the night?" Harris hunched down in his coat. "Why can't we riddle the place with bullets and be done with it?"

"It's supposed to look like an accident. Clog the

chimney, crank up the gas, however you do it, it had better not come back on me." He rolled up the window, turned the key in the ignition, and headed down the mountain, grateful for the snow chains that would enable him to get home and back.

He really didn't care how, or when, Harris disposed of those inside the house. He only wanted to make sure Harris died, too. For that to happen, he needed to wait for the group from St. Louis to finish arriving. His plan of rival gangs fighting over a prosperous marijuana farm was sheer genius.

It wouldn't be hard to plant a bug in a few law enforcement ears that one DEA, John Canyon, was dirty and on the take.

CHAPTER TWENTY-ONE

T he snow stopped falling by ten p.m. The moon cast a blue pall over the land and highlighted the men in black marring the pristine landscape.

Lacey stepped back from the window. She'd taken several photos of the men out front. Hopefully, it would be enough to identify them. The inactivity set her nerves on edge. While she didn't want a gunfight, she did want an end to the standoff. She turned and studied John's face as he spoke to his supervisor.

"Tell me how many men are out there," he told Lacey.

She peered out and counted. "There were five, now there are eight. More arrived when the snow stopped." She set her camera on the fireplace mantel. "It's hard to see their faces, but the authorities should be able to zoom in."

He spoke the information into the phone. "I don't know how long they'll pace. I'm expecting action at any time. We need help." He frowned. "That long? I hope we're alive by then." He hung up and glanced at the others. "Minimum of three hours."

Lacey's shoulders slumped. "I'll make coffee. Thank goodness this house has a gas stove."

Except for Meagan, who was blissfully unaware of the danger, the others wouldn't sleep. She checked on the little girl, who lay on a quilt on the living room floor. She sucked her thumb. Lacey smiled and smoothed her hair out of her face.

Lawson sat on the sofa, the white bandage in stark contrast to his dark skin. His head was back, eyes closed. She doubted he slept, but it was good he rested. After helping John cart the wood for the windows, he'd trembled like a scared puppy.

"How are you holding up?" John slipped an arm around her waist.

"Fine." She leaned into him, relishing his touch. From the moment she'd met him, they'd been pursued by danger. How could she have fallen so deeply in love over the span of a few weeks?

She tilted her head. "Kiss me."

He grinned. "Now? Why?"

What man asked questions after a demand like that? She ran a finger over his lips. "If I die, I don't want it to be before I've been kissed by you."

He lowered his head and pulled her close, his mouth close to hers. "Then, I'll make it a kiss you can take with you to heaven." He claimed her lips.

Send her to heaven more likely. He stole her breath and made her knees weak. She slipped her arms around his neck and held on, pressing closer. His kiss gave her hope they'd survive. It held the promise of more to come … someday. When she couldn't breathe, she pulled away and rested her cheek on his chest, counting his heartbeats.

His hold on her tightened and he rested his chin on her head. "We will survive this, Lacey. God would tell me." He sighed. "Jason knew he was going to die. Said he saw it in a dream. He heard God telling him He was going to call him and Michelle home. I shrugged it off, but now … I believe him. And, God hasn't done anything more than show me a future with you and Meagan. Do you believe that?"

"I want to." With everything in her, she wanted to believe.

"If the two of you are done being mushy, I'm trying to get some rest," Lawson said. He opened one eye. "If things go south, you're going to need me. Right now, I'm as helpless as that little girl."

Lacey's face flamed. "Sorry." She took John's hand and pulled him into the hall. Giggling, she leaned her forehead against his shoulder. "I forgot he was there."

John tilted her face to his. "I promised to take care of you. Do you trust me?"

She nodded.

"Do you trust me to see that justice is done so you don't have to hold so tightly to revenge?"

"Yes. I trust you, and God, to see this through. But, a fist of fear has hold of me and won't let go. I can't shake the feeling that something bad is going to happen to you."

"Have faith, sweet—"

A crashing through the window, a curse from Lawson, and a shrill scream from Meagan had them running back into the living room. A smoke grenade billowed from the center of the room. Lacey snatched the little girl, quilt and all, from the floor and rushed with her to the kitchen.

How had they gotten the grenade inside? Were they so brazen they'd shove it through the two inches of space left for John and Lawson to shoot through?

John thundered into the kitchen, his shirt over his nose, his eyes red. "We shoved it back outside, but they're surrounding the house. Please." He cupped Lacey's face. "Take Meagan to the whiskey room and stay there."

"I can help."

"Please. You don't have the experience the rest of us have. I need you to watch my niece. Keep her safe." He shoved her gun into her hands.

"All right." She whirled and dashed away as a thundering noise came from the front porch.

Inside the hidden room, she closed the door. Complete darkness surrounded her. She sat Meagan on the floor and felt for a lamp. She found one on the table, a box of matches next to it. Someone had thought of everything, even bottles of water and packages of peanut butter and cheese crackers. A thick quilt was folded in the corner. She lit an oil lamp and turned the wick low, then sat against the dirt wall, a crying Meagan in her lap, and prayed harder than she had ever prayed in her life.

~

John's eyes streamed tears down his face. He'd gotten the neckline of his shirt up fast, but not fast enough. From outside, the grenade still poured smoke into the room.

Alice handed him and Lawson small paper masks

that covered their nose and mouth, then handed them both a rifle. "There are four of them in back."

That left four in front. "I'll take the front. Lawson, you take the back. Alice, you go wherever the greatest need is." John took a deep breath. "And pray. I made a promise to Lacey that I intend to keep."

Lawson nodded. "Here goes nothing, folks. I hope the calvary arrives soon." He took up his position at the back door.

"Me, too." John headed for the living room, fighting not to check on Lacey and Meagan. They were safe down below. Far safer than he was.

"Come out and you'll be allowed to live," Harris bellowed through a megaphone.

Right. Because John was an idiot. "I'm not going to make your job easy, Harris!"

A curse drifted from the corner of the house. "Then prepare to die."

Dramatic. John leaned against the wall of the house, keeping an eye on the three men standing at the edge of the road. Seconds later, Harris trudged through the snow and joined them. *Thank you, God, for a full moon.* It would be a nightmare if the clouds didn't part.

He sent his boss a text, letting him know things were escalating, then settled back to wait. Let Harris or one of his goons fire the first shot.

A truck pulled up and Ben Harper climbed out. He marched over to Harris, waved his arms around, then stomped back to his truck. Was the fat cop not following directions?

"What are they waiting for?" Alice held out a mug of hot coffee. "Are they going to try and kill us or not?"

He shrugged and accepted the drink. "It seems as if

the boss man and the hired help are having a disagreement."

"Maybe they'll shoot each other and spare us the trouble." She grinned and left the room.

John chuckled. Alice was a rare find. Tiny, but mighty, with a tongue that could cut steel. He was glad she was on his side.

"I got movement in the back," Lawson called. "They're ducking behind the stack of wood and taking aim."

"Heads up," John said. "This is it."

A shot rang out from the back. Lawson yelled as the bullet struck the side of the house. "My grandpap built this place solid."

"Good thing." John took aim out his window and squeezed the trigger. His first shot flattened a tire on Harper's truck. The second went through the leg of a man who didn't have the sense to hide when the first shot rang out.

Men cursed and dove for cover. Within minutes, shots struck the house with the rapidity of popcorn. John hit the floor. When the shots quieted, he resumed his position and took aim at Harris. His next shot felled the fat man like a bag of horse feed.

The next shot at the house found its way through the two inches between the window frame and the plywood and ripped through John's shoulder. Another, took him in the side. He whirled like a marionette before falling. He managed to shout for Alice before blackness fought to overtake him. The shattered remains of his coffee mug lay beside him.

"I've got it." Alice took up his position. "Stay awake."

"I'm trying." He shook his head to rid himself of the dizziness and scooted against the fireplace. "Give me a minute, and I'll be back at my post."

"I got it." She fired a shot, then clutched her arm and cried out. "I'm hit."

"Go get Lacey." As much as he hated to say it, they needed her to fight. "Wrap your arm and guard my niece."

"I can still shoot."

"Please." Nausea threatened to make him lose his dinner. From the pain and the thought of Lacey being where the danger was.

As Alice stumbled from the room, John crawled back to the window and resumed his position. His legs trembled, but he fought against the weakness and aimed his rifle.

"Sit down." Lacey pushed him out of the way and took the gun. "Don't be a fool." She squeezed off a shot. "One down. One more to go."

He shook his head at her strength. He knew she'd come through in a pinch. *Please, God, don't let her bravery result in her death.*

"Missed." She ducked and reloaded.

"Where did you learn to shoot like that?"

"My grandfather. Of course, that was at tin cans, and I miss more than I hit. Darn. Missed again. Hold still, right there—got him!" Still holding the gun, she dashed for the kitchen.

John closed his eyes and slid down the wall.

~

Ben stared down at Harris, who clutched his gut. The man was belly-shot. He wouldn't last long. Ben took aim with his pistol and put a bullet between the man's eyes.

He stared at the carnage around him. Only one other man besides Harris lay dead, but the others were too wounded to fight further. Ben cursed and stared at the house. They needed to die. Now. The games were over.

He raced across the snow and plastered his back against the side of the house. There had to be an opening somewhere. He fiddled with the lighter in his pocket. There was a shed in the back. Most likely a fuel can inside. He'd burn them out.

The moon lit his path as he ran across the yard. The shed was unlocked. He squeezed inside and used the light streaming through a small window to locate a can of kerosene. Smiling, he soaked several cleaning rags lying on a work bench, then gathered them up. Placed under the broken front window, the fire would spread inside quickly and flush those inside out like rabbits.

The cold seeped through his thin shoes and jacket. He needed to hurry before his fingers refused to work.

He lit the rags, then tossed them one by one onto the porch. It wouldn't be long now. He couldn't wait to stare into Lacey's frightened face as he pulled the trigger and got rid of the worse thorn in his side he'd ever had. Why couldn't she accept Ruth's death as an accident and move on?

As he sprinted back to his truck, a spotlight landed on him. He glanced up into the face of a soldier hanging from a helicopter. The soldier stared impassively at Ben and aimed his gun.

CHAPTER TWENTY-TWO

As a helicopter thumped overhead, Lacey slid down the wall to sit splay-legged on the floor next to an unconscious John. She glanced at what remained of her camera, lying in pieces on the floor.

Lawson staggered into the room and collapsed on the sofa. "Alice is wounded pretty bad," he said. "A guy riddled the back door with bullets. One caught her in the leg and another in the side."

"I told her to go down with Lacey. Why don't women listen better?"

"We're stubborn. I need to check on Meagan." Lacey tried to push to her feet, doing her best to ignore the pain in her side from a bullet graze of her own.

"I'll get her." He pushed to his feet and staggered from the room, returning minutes later with a sleeping toddler in his arms. He placed her gently on the sofa. "I wish I could sleep through danger."

Lacey gave him a sad smile and crawled to John's

side. His breathing was shallow, but he breathed, which meant he lived. She took his hand in hers and stroked the back of it. He'd lost so much blood, tried so hard to keep fighting, only to succumb when she had enough of hiding and joined the fray.

"He wanted to protect me," she said. "Looks like the roles were reversed."

"I doubt he'd be alive if you'd listened to him and stayed below," Lawson said. "I'm going to bring Alice in here. I don't want her to regain consciousness alone, and her wounds need bandaged."

Lacey wasn't a nurse, not even close, but she'd do what she could. She snapped John's pocket knife off his belt and started cutting up towels Alice had washed and folded the day before. When she cut a strip, she tied it around a bullet wound. When she'd finished with John and Alice, they both wore multi-colored terry strips as badges of honor.

"Let me wrap your side." Lawson propped Alice in a chair, then grabbed a salmon-colored strip. "The house is in sad shape. Your house is burned down. What are you going to do now?"

She hissed against the pain of him pulling the bandage tight. "Whatever John wants to do."

Someone pounded on the front door. "This is Stephen Mansfield. Anyone able to open the door?"

"Hold on." Lawson patted Lacey's cheek. "You did good, kid. I wasn't sure you had it in you."

"Neither did I." She knelt back by John's side. "The cavalry is here."

His eyes fluttered open as Lawson let Mansfield in. "About … time."

A short, balding man with dark eyes that darted

around the room before focusing on Lacey, stepped through the door. "There's a lot of bodies outside and a lot of wounded in here." He stepped aside as emergency personnel rushed in. "Anyone dead?"

"No." Lawson identified himself.

Paramedics laughed at the strange, but effective wound dressings, before placing Alice and John on gurneys. They wheeled Alice out first, leaving Lacey to scoop the drowsy Meagan into her arms. *Thank you, God, for sparing this child.* Things could have gone really bad.

"You're hurt." John grabbed her arm.

"I'm fine." She smiled down at him. "Mine is just a graze."

"Thank you for not listening to me."

"You might as well get used to it. I'm not going anywhere."

John reached up from the gurney and cupped her face. "I love you. Marry me as soon as I'm on my feet."

She leaned into his touch. "Don't you want to spend some time getting to know me better?"

"I know all I need to know."

She bent and kissed him. "Then, yes, I'll marry you. From the hospital bed if you want."

"I'd rather stand while you walk down the aisle."

She walked alongside him as the paramedics wheeled him to the ambulance. Off to the side, she spotted Ben being shoved into a waiting squad car. She handed Meagan to an officer and marched to Ben.

"Why?" She waved around at the bodies being zipped into bags. "Was it worth it?"

"No." He scowled. "You're still alive."

Tears clogged her throat. "Why was it so important

for you to kill me?"

"Blame it on your aunt's nosiness. The two of you ruined the Harper family."

"No, you did that back in 1929 when you hung an innocent man." She smiled as sweetly as she could. "I forgive you, Ben Harper. For everything."

Feeling lighter than she had in months, Lacey climbed into the ambulance with a sleeping John and set Meagan back on her lap. She was going to marry the man lying in front of her. She'd be a wife and a mother.

Tears ran down her face. It was a hard journey getting here, but she'd arrived.

"Are you in pain?" One of the medical personnel peered into her face.

Lacey shook her head. "I've never felt better." She buried her face in Meagan's hair and continued to cry.

Without opening his eyes, John reached for her hand. "Silly woman."

She entwined her fingers with his. "More like lucky woman." She kissed the back of his hand. "I love you, John Canyon."

"I love you, Lacey Baxter." He opened one eye and gave her a dimpled smile. "I'll show you how much once I'm able to stand."

"I'm looking forward to it." Lacey Canyon. She liked the sound of it.

The End

ABOUT THE AUTHOR

Website at www.cynthiahickey.com
Also www.forgetmenotromances.com

Multi-published and Amazon Best-Selling author Cynthia Hickey had three cozy mysteries and two novellas published through Barbour Publishing. Her first mystery, Fudge-Laced Felonies, won first place in the inspirational category of the Great Expectations contest in 2007. Her third cozy, Chocolate-Covered Crime, received a four-star review from Romantic Times. All three cozies have been re-released as ebooks through the MacGregor Literary Agency, along with a new cozy series, all of which stay in the top 50 of Amazon's ebooks for their genre. She had several historical romances release through Harlequin's Heartsong Presents, and has sold close to a million copies of her works since 2013. She has taught a Continuing Education class at the 2015 American Christian Fiction Writers conference. You can find her on FB, twitter, and Goodreads, and is a contributor to Cozy Mystery Magazine blog and Suspense Sisters blog. She and her husband run the small press, Forget Me Not Romances, which includes some of the CBA's best well-known authors. She lives in Arizona with her husband, one of their seven children, two dogs, two cats, three box turtles, and two Sulcata tortoises. She has seven grandchildren who keep her busy and tell everyone they know that "Nana is a writer".